For Fox Sake

MARY FRAME

Book Cover by Qamber Designs

https://www.qamberdesignsmedia.com/

Content edits by Catherine Felnagle

Copy edits by Elizabeth Nover at Razor Sharp Editing

www.razorsharpediting.com

To my namesake and aunt, Mary Susan Humphrey. Gone too soon, but never forgotten.

Description

Jake Fox is a man on a mission. Armed with a collection of mysterious letters between his late father and a stranger named Ryan, Jake wants nothing more than to unravel the enigma: Just who is this Ryan guy? But when Jake arrives in Dull, Oregon, he finds Ryan is no *guy* at all.

Ryan Green is just trying to get by. So while the handsome stranger who pays for her groceries intrigues her, caring for her dying mom and raising her dead sister's daughter are all she has time for. But when the muscular handyman moves in across the street, the spark of their chemistry is difficult to ignore.

Safe in the blue-eyed beauty's company, Jake can't quite confront his past—or share his true purpose in Oregon.

But the deeper Ryan falls, the closer their intertwined histories come to splitting them apart.

For Fox Sake is the poignant fifth book in the Fox Family romantic comedy series and can be read as a stand-alone, but the experience is definitely enhanced by starting with book one: *Between a Fox and a Hard Place*!

If you like witty characters, swoony moments, and grief leavened with humor, then you'll adore this heartfelt tale of love, loss, and the complexities of unraveling the past.

Chapter One

RYAN

"But *why*?"

Twenty-seven. That's twenty-seven times Ari has asked me *why?* since this morning.

It started as soon as she opened her eyes.

Why can't I go with you to work?

Why do we have cereal for breakfast? Why can't I have pizza?

Why do I have two eyes if I can only see one thing?

"Because you've worn your superhero cape for three days straight. It's covered in dirt and old food and every germ known to humankind. We're going into a place where they sell food, which means we have to be clean so dirt doesn't get on all the stuff people are gonna eat."

The parking lot is clear of traffic as I grip Ari's hand tighter and cross to the store entrance.

She's silent for two whole seconds before saying, "But the rest of me isn't clean either."

Sighing, I release her sticky hand to grab a cart. She's not wrong. This round goes to the five-year-old for an unerring sense of logic that exists only when it's the least useful for me.

Her ruffled pink skirt is speckled with red and yellow paint. Pale blue streaks haphazardly across her white shirt. The perfectly styled braids I wove into her hair this morning have worked free, and blond curls riot around her face. Her mouth is surrounded by some of the same pale blue substance from her shirt, tinted with grayish grime. That's what happens when you feed a child ice pops before they play outside in the dirt.

"Just don't touch anything."

"But—"

My purse vibrates. "Hold on."

Saved by the bell, or some disaster, more likely. But whatever. It's an opportunity to distract us both from this no-win conversation.

I lift my phone out of my purse with one hand, pushing the cart forward with the other. We stop just inside the door, moving to the side to let a couple behind us pass.

The caller ID flashes. It's Priscilla. Crap.

I swipe my thumb across the screen. "Hey. Everything all right?"

"Where are you?" Pricilla asks.

"BountiDull Foods." When you live in a town named Dull, the puns are both frequent and terrible. "What's going on?"

"Uh, so, one of the last renters left a little something behind."

"What is it?"

"Crabs."

Ari stares up at me and frowns at my expression. "Momma?"

My brain stalls out for a second. Crabs? *Crabs*? Live crabs?"

"You wouldn't freaking believe it. I opened the fridge and there they were, free-roaming like they owned the place."

Dull is only an hour from a prime crab-catching area along the Tillamook. We get a lot of renters here for that kind of thing, but no one has ever left their live catch behind before.

"Are you fu—uh, kidding me?"

Thankfully Ari's not paying attention. She's waving at someone deeper into the store, toward the apple bins.

I twist around to look.

Priscilla's gusty sigh echoes across the line. "I need some help getting them out. You know how I feel about spiders."

"Crabs aren't spiders." I move the phone away from my mouth and whisper to Ari, "Who are you waving at?"

"They're sea spiders," Priscilla's voice continues in

3

my ear. "All those legs twitching about gives me the creeps. And they're larger and scarier."

Ari's eyes brighten. "Can I see the crabs?"

"No."

"What?" Priscilla asks.

"Not you. I'm with Ari. Which unit are you cleaning?" *Please don't be 2E.*

"2E."

I groan and lift a hand to my head. That's the one right across the street from our home. "It's booked for three weeks and check-in starts in," I inspect my watch, "ten minutes." Which doesn't mean they will show up right then, but you never know.

"What do you want me to do?"

Ari tugs on my arm. "I want to see the crabs."

I shake my head and blow out a breath. What is with today?

My period started this morning, I've been putting out one fire after another at the rentals, and I had the worst lunch date in the history of the known universe.

"Give me ten minutes. Take care of whatever else needs to be done until then." I hang up, narrowing my eyes at Ari. "I'll let you look at the crabs if you let me wash your cape."

Her head cocks to one side, lips pursing, like we're bargaining for her soul instead of the state of her personal hygiene. "Okay."

"Did you want some strawberries?"

"No. Bananas."

I guide the cart in that direction. "Who were you waving at earlier?"

"Uncle Shane."

Fucking hell.

I immediately hunch, my eyes darting around us, like there's a sniper hiding behind the pineapples instead of my ex-boyfriend.

It's not like I never see him. We run into each other at least once a week.

I hate small towns.

Maybe it's just this small town. Too many memories.

"Hey, Ryan."

I spin around.

Shane's dark hair is slicked back, one hand stuffed into his jeans pocket, the other holding his girlfriend's hand.

She flicks her blond hair and smirks at me. Samantha. I barely know her, but what I do know is she's one of those people who wields backhanded compliments like a weapon.

"Hey, Shane. Hey, Sam."

Her mouth twists. "It's Samantha."

"Right, sorry. How are you?"

"We're doing great, actually." Samantha rests her left hand on her lower stomach to show off the flashing diamond engagement ring, her smile widening. "We're expecting."

My mouth pops open and I snap it shut. "Wow. That's, that's great. Congratulations."

Samantha's smirk is smug. She didn't miss my initial reaction, and she probably thinks I'm jealous.

This doesn't hurt in the way she thinks it does. I'm way over Shane. Even though we were together for years, we've been over longer than we were together.

He's grinning down at her, and it's just . . . so *weird*.

Samantha yaps on and on, about how they are trying to maintain a healthier diet now that she's eating for two, how they have a doctor's appointment next week, how they're already picking out baby names and she likes Darcy for a girl and Toby for a boy.

I nod and tune out.

Shane puts an arm around her shoulders and gazes down at her like she's the most interesting person alive.

He used to look at me the same way. In public, anyway. Shane puts on this act like he's this fun-loving, great guy, attentive and sensitive. Every time we see him, he insists Ari call him "uncle" since he "was there when she was born." While he may have been physically present, he was a complete asshat. He refused to help me with any of Ari's care, even though we were living together, my only sister had just died, and I was drowning in grief.

Honestly, they're perfect for each other.

"I'm really happy for both of you. It was so nice to chat. We have to run though. We're kind of in a hurry."

"We have crabs," Ari pipes up.

I laugh awkwardly and shrug as we're walking away. "Kids say the funniest things."

Five minutes later, we've finished a frenzied race through the store for the basics to last the next few days and then we get in line. We're behind three people with full carts. Two more quickly fall into place behind us.

Only one register open on a Friday night. Of course.

After interminable minutes standing in line while I try to distract and entertain Ari, it's finally our turn.

"That will be twenty-three forty-five," the cashier says, after scanning the last item in our basket.

I reach into my purse and dig around, my fingers encountering my phone, the car keys, a travel-size pack of tissues, Chapstick, a bag of almonds, and hand sanitizer.

Frowning, I tug the bag from my shoulder and peer inside.

My fingers are not deceiving me.

No wallet.

"Shit."

"That's a bad word," Ari tells me.

"Sorry, baby. Um, I think I left my wallet in the car." I turn to the cashier, a teenager with bright green streaks in her hair. She's chewing gum and eyeballing the ever-growing line behind me.

"Can I run out real quick and check?" My face is so hot right now it might burst into flames like the head of a struck match.

I can't believe this is happening.

When did I last use my wallet? Was it earlier when I paid for lunch during my terrible date? Or maybe it fell out when I was answering my phone. Maybe it's in the car somewhere. What am I going to do if I can't find it? I'm going to have to take Ari with me while I'm searching everywhere, all while she asks me *why* a thousand more times, and if I can't find it—

"I've got this." A deep voice behind me breaks through my racing thoughts. A tanned and toned forearm reaches across the register and hands a plastic card to the cashier.

The limb pulls back to its owner.

Its extremely attractive owner.

Fuck my life.

He has dark hair pushed back from his head, disheveled like he's been running his fingers through it, or he just rolled out of bed.

Our eyes meet, his warm and brown, mine stressed, humiliated, and exhausted. My mortification rises as I absorb his striking features: aquiline nose and strong chin accentuated by scruff lining his jaw.

I'm painfully aware of my own plain brown hair, cut short because it's the easiest and most efficient style, the lack of makeup on my face, and the dirt smudging my shirt. I had to help Priscilla pull some weeds after lunch and I never had a chance to change or clean up or refresh my deodorant.

And now this handsome stranger is paying for my food.

I swallow the shame of it down long enough to speak. "Thank you so much. I'm so sorry. I can pay you back."

"It's nothing, really."

"Seriously, if you give me your information, I'll get the money to you as soon as possible."

"Don't worry about it." The corner of his mouth kicks up and every female in a fifty-foot radius sighs.

Except Ari.

"Momma," she says, tugging on my arm. "I have to poop."

I sigh. "That about sums up my whole day perfectly."

Hot Guy barks out a laugh.

I give him a wry smile while dying inside.

Why me?

The crab problem ends up being the easiest part of my day. We're able to capture them by opening the fridge just wide enough to hold up a cooler and corral them inside. It only takes ten minutes because eventually, the suckers crawl right in. Priscilla only releases three blood-curdling screams during the whole process.

We avoid having to explain the situation to the renter, because he still hasn't arrived by the time Ari and I leave with the cooler, taking it out to the nearest river to release the crabs.

Three hours later, I finally get a little peace and quiet.

I sit on the old beige couch in my living room with two packages of fruit snacks and take a deep breath, slumping back against cushions soft from years of use.

Ari is finally asleep. Dinner was chicken strips, fries, and fruit salad because I only had enough bandwidth to open and shut the oven.

Then it was bath time, followed by letting Ari watch a half hour of *Bluey* before bedtime.

But that's never the end of it. She got up twice to go to the bathroom and another time to get a drink of water.

The girl is always thirstiest at nine p.m.

But now, finally, the house is silent. I've put in a load of laundry, including Ari's cape, and now it's time to unwind. My mind circles back, recapping the events of the day.

I can't believe Samantha is pregnant.

I can't believe people left live freaking crabs in a rental.

I can't believe I lost my wallet and some hot guy bought me groceries today.

I can't believe I went on the worst lunch date ever and that tragic event was the highlight of my day.

Demolishing the first package of fruit snacks, I crumple the wrapper and toss it on the coffee table.

Maybe the highlight of my day was the brief moment with the guy at the store, despite the embarrassment of not being able to pay for our food. He was really hot. And obviously generous. I bet he doesn't chew with his mouth open like the guy I went to lunch with earlier. Or more likely, he does.

If life has taught me anything, it's that fantasy is

always better than reality. If I got to know him, I would probably find out he's a liar, player, bigot, sociopath, or some combination of all four, like every other guy I've attempted to date in the past six years . . . which to be fair is like, two, but whatever.

I take a deep breath and blow it out. I love this time of night. It's the only time I have to relax.

The doorbell rings, and I jump to my feet.

I pass the hall to the bedrooms on my way to the front door, ears straining for the patter of Ari's feet. Once she's out, she's a deep sleeper, but still. This better not be one of the tenants. It shouldn't be. Our address isn't listed on anything, only my number for emergencies before nine. After nine, it rings to Priscilla since I can't leave Ari.

I stretch up on my toes to peer through the peephole. Surprise knocks me back on my heels. What the hell is he doing here?

Pulling the door open, I step out on the porch and shut the door behind me.

"Ryan. You're home." Rob's eyes flick up and down my body and my skin crawls.

I threw on sweats and a tank top when Ari and I were doing our bedtime routine. It is not a sexy look, so why is he checking me out like that? I cross my arms over my chest.

Why is my terrible lunch date here? How did he get my address?

"What are you doing here?" Behind him, an unfamiliar gray sedan is parked in front of my house. That must be his car.

Across the street, in front of the newly dubbed "crab shack," a single light is on in the front window and an old green pickup rests dark and silent against the curb. The renter made it.

The rest of the cul-de-sac is dark and empty.

He holds up a square black object. "You left this at the restaurant."

My wallet. Relief surges through me. "Oh thank god." I pluck it from his fingers and flip it open, checking everything inside is intact.

Rob leans in and lifts a hand, pressing his palm flat against the doorframe near my head. "What? You think I would steal from you?"

"Oh, no, of course not. I just wanted to make sure nothing fell out, or I didn't leave my card in the billfold at the restaurant. I've done that before."

"I didn't even look in there. Well, except to get the address so I could find you." He leans closer, his breath fanning my face.

Ugh. He stinks like stale beer.

The chicken strips from dinner curdle in my stomach.

He's not bad looking. He's thirty, single, blond, and blue eyed, and he has a good job. He just started working with my best friend's brother at his contracting company building houses. He's some kind of engineer, so he's smart. On paper, he's great.

In reality? Not so much.

During our date, he talked about himself nonstop, forgot his wallet, chewed with his mouth open, and checked his phone every time I opened my mouth to contribute to the conversation.

Not to mention that while he did bring me my wallet and didn't steal from me, he also hasn't offered to pay me back for his half of lunch. And why did he wait until nine o'clock at night to bring me my wallet?

He leans in closer. "Are you going to invite me in?"

Ah ha. That's why. He thought I might fall to my knees in gratitude. Literally. Ick. "No."

"No?" He blinks, as if baffled by the word.

"It's not a good time." Not that I need to explain myself. *No* is a complete sentence, after all.

His brow wrinkles and his gaze slides to the door behind me, like he can see through the wood. "Do you have someone else here?"

"No."

As if to immediately contradict my words, a thump sounds behind me, and the handle turns.

"Momma?"

I flip around, attempting to block her view. I don't introduce men I date to Ari. Not that there have been many of them, but I wouldn't even think about it until I've vetted them thoroughly and I know it might go somewhere. I only do one-off lunch dates when she's in school or camp and not around to see it.

"Stay inside, baby. I'll be right in."

She frowns but is too groggy to argue with me or ask who's here or *why*, thankfully.

I shut the door.

Rob is sneering at me, his lip curling in disdain. "You have a kid?"

"Yes. I have a kid." My eyes flick to the scooter resting against the porch railing, then the Barbie Mermaid pool in the corner and the container of sidewalk chalk next to it.

This guy is a moron.

I straighten, squaring my shoulders. "It's time for you to leave."

"Whatever." He waves a hand behind him, already stomping down the porch steps. "I can't believe Austin thought I would be into used goods," he mutters as he's walking away.

I roll my eyes and grit my teeth, taking a deep breath before slipping back inside, locking the door behind me, and hitting the porch light off with a little more force than necessary.

"Who was that, Momma?" Ari peers at me from the hallway.

"No one. No one at all." I pick her up, her head dropping to my shoulder as her sleepy warmth wraps around me.

"The talking woke me up," she mutters into my neck.

"It's okay. No more talking."

I carry her back to her room and tuck her in, her eyes remaining shut the whole time. I sit on the edge of her bed and watch her for a minute. A soft blue glow from her Elsa night light shines over her face, her long eyelashes casting crescent shadows on her cheeks.

I wouldn't give up my life, as challenging as it can be, for anything. Definitely not for some douchebag who doesn't even know how to chew food properly.

Anyone who sees a child as baggage and not as a gift isn't worth my time or energy.

I suppose it's a good thing that the trash takes itself out, every single time.

Chapter Two

JAKE

Seconds after the porch light goes off at the house across the street, I drop the curtain. I didn't intend to spy, but when a car door slammed outside, I couldn't resist. I've never had a neighbor before. I've never lived anywhere outside of my family's sprawling property, where the nearest neighbor is a mile away.

Then once I started, I couldn't stop. The woman who answered the door looked a whole hell of a lot like the woman from the store. Her tension was palpable, even with a street between us.

I couldn't tell if I needed to intervene. I kept watching just in case I needed to run out there if things escalated.

Who was he? An ex-boyfriend?

Earlier, at the store, she was flustered and distressed, her face bright red with embarrassment.

And yet she kept it together and retained her sense of humor in an awkward situation. Even cracked a joke when her little girl said she had to poop.

I chuckle.

She had dirt on her clothes and violet smudges under her eyes. But her eyes were bright and intelligent, and she had this almost glow about her that—

Holy hell, I sound like a damn teen drama.

I blame my sisters for forcing me into hours and hours of *Grey's Anatomy* and *Vampire Diaries*, which I absolutely did not enjoy even though technically I could have left the room at any time.

Anyway. It doesn't matter because I'm only here temporarily and I have more important things to focus on.

I walk over to the desk in the corner where the informational booklet on the rental is propped open. I run a finger down the page until it lands on the name and contact info for the property manager, the person I've been stalking for over a year now, and the reason I left my hometown of Whitby, New York, to spend time in Dull, Oregon.

Ryan Green.

My cell phone rings and I groan. I've been avoiding most of my calls, mostly from my sister Finley and her fiancé Archer, but I can't avoid this one.

If I don't answer, he'll come after me.

In reality, he'll pay other people to come after me. Lots of people. As many as it takes. He has the resources and connections to send in the CIA, probably.

I take a deep breath, forcing myself to relax and answer. "Hey, Oliver."

"You need to call Finley."

Getting right to the point, as usual, his voice snapping like a disgruntled turtle. It's cute. He's worried about me.

I tread down the short hallway to the bedroom, using the time to pause for a few long seconds, just to be annoying. "I'm doing great, thanks for asking. How are you?"

"I didn't invest that money for you to take off without a word to your sisters."

"I left word."

Nine words, to be precise. On a sticky note I pressed to the fridge as I was walking out the door.

Went to look for letter writer. I'll be back.

It was succinct. To the point. Poetic, even. Maybe a Haiku. I scratch my head. How many syllables are needed for a Haiku?

"I never should have told you about the money."

"Uh, pretty sure it would have been illegal not to, my bro."

Oliver practically growls. He's probably strangling his cell phone at this point.

I grin at the thought and pick up my bag from the

floor, setting it on the pale green bedspread and rummaging for sleep clothes.

Over a year ago, I began sending Oliver a large chunk of my paychecks to invest for me. Out of nowhere, he called me last month to tell me he'd quadrupled my investment—and it continues to grow. He's got a golden thumb. He's good at everything. He never loses, ever. He wins every competition I can think of, from fishing to axe throwing to goddamn cross-stitching. It doesn't matter what it is. The man is like a medical marvel. It's annoying. But also convenient for me, since I needed the money to spend a couple of weeks investigating. So I can't be too petty. At least, not outwardly.

"I am not your bro," he huffs.

"You will be soon enough."

He's more or less my brother-in-law because even if he hasn't married Piper yet, it's only a matter of time.

Where are my pajama pants? My fingers wrap around something silky, and I tug it loose from the jumble of clothes in my bag.

I lift it up. It's a black V-neck tee that is at least three sizes too small. And a crop top. And there's a rhinestone raccoon bedazzled on the front with the words *Trash Panda* glittering across the chest.

This is Finley's shirt.

I sigh and chuck it on the bed. Archer bought her that shirt as a gift for Christmas. They are so weird. It must have gotten mixed up in my laundry. What is it with them and raccoons? I don't understand the fascination. They're a menace and they look like corgis who've gone emo.

"Is this about your dad's letters?" Oliver asks.

"Yes."

"What is your plan?"

I'm not prepared to share everything I know, which isn't much.

My plan is to find the truth, the answers to the questions that have been plaguing me for months.

Did Dad have a second family? Why did he hide this relationship from us? What even is this relationship? Who exchanges letters back and forth for months with a total stranger? If it's just a meaningless pen pal, why hide it? It's like he had this whole second life. Why didn't he tell us? Why didn't he tell *me*?

We were so close, especially near the end of his life, when I was his primary caretaker. We talked a lot. About everything. Well, almost everything.

He was one of the few people who understood the one topic I avoided and why.

And I thought I understood him. But for the past year and a half, I haven't known what to think.

"What about the camp? Don't they need you?" Oliver's voice in my ear rips me from my thoughts.

"Finley hired enough counselors to babysit half the kids in upstate New York." It was always a pity job anyway, since my sister is the majority owner of the property where the kids camp is located, a property that has been in our family forever. Oliver is the other stakeholder and the one who funded the charitable venture.

"Where are you?" Oliver asks.

I scratch the back of my head. "I'm not quite ready to elaborate on that."

"You know I have the means to find out."

I snort. I'm sure. He probably has a dozen gray-hat hackers on retainer. "You won't have to. I'll be back in a few weeks. This is something I need to do on my own."

"I'm not going to lie to Piper."

"I'm not asking you to. You don't know where I am. You have plausible deniability."

"If she asks me to send out the search party, I'm not saying no."

I sigh. I can argue with him, but that will be as useful as arguing with a park bench. "Just don't do anything until she asks, okay?"

"Fine." The line clicks.

He hung up.

I chuckle at the phone and then toss it on the bed.

That will buy me some time at least. Hopefully enough time to get what I need and get back to Whitby before my family descends. I had to leave. The walls were closing in. Every time Finley looked at me with that divot between her brow and a frown tugging at her mouth, I wanted to bolt. Or drink. And drinking isn't an option.

Archer and Finley were constantly hovering, asking if I was okay, searching my face with concerned eyes—not exactly heinous behavior, but I'm twenty-seven years old.

They need to realize I can handle things. That I can stand on my own. I'm not perfect, and I'm not entirely over . . . everything that's happened in the past. I'll never stop grieving, but I'm fine. I'm surviving. They don't need to hold on so tight. Any tighter, I might crack.

But now that I think of it, leaving with no word except that one Post-it may not have been the best way to stop their worrying. But what else could I do? They would never stand aside while I did this on my own.

I zip my bag closed before dumping it on the floor beside the bed again. The house is small, the bedroom barely large enough to fit the queen-sized bed and dresser, but it's clean and well maintained.

It could have been a complete hovel and I would've booked it. I picked this place because of the property manager.

Ryan Green.

A year and a half ago, my siblings and I went through our dad's bedroom together to clean it out and found a stack of letters to our dad from someone named Ryan. Most of the letters were stories and updates about someone named Mia. None of us knew who these people were. My sisters didn't want to know. They had their own stuff going on.

For months, I read through the letters, hunting for clues, trying to figure out the connection or any hints at all as to who these people were and why they were writing to Dad.

There was a phrase that didn't quite make sense, *good*

old Dull. I thought it was a mistake or some lingo or slang I just wasn't getting, but then I realized there's a town called Dull in Oregon.

Once I had that little clue, I hired a private investigator, Dwayne, to help me find Ryan and Mia. That was all I had to go on, no last names, nothing else specific, but it's a small town so it didn't take long to find them.

Within weeks, Dwayne located an obituary for Mia. She died six years ago. She was only twenty-one. The article listed her surviving relatives, including a sibling named Ryan Green. It has to be him, the letter writer.

I've had a year plus forty-one hours of solo drive time to come up with some ideas on how to find out the truth.

Objective number one: find a way to meet Ryan. It started with renting this property he manages. I don't know where he lives, but I have his contact information. Then, once we're face-to-face, I'll . . . I have no idea.

The most logical approach would be to ask why he was writing to my dad, but what if he's my brother? What if he's not? I need to see him in person and get an idea of what kind of person he is. Then maybe I'll know what path to take forward. The only thing I know for certain is I need a DNA sample. Maybe that will clear some things up without a confrontation.

Across the room, the box my PI sent me rests atop the dresser. It's a small, prestamped package with all the materials needed to send in a DNA sample. They'll even do a rush job and get me the results within a couple of days. For a fee, of course.

Based on research Dwayne conducted through my ancestry records, there's no obvious genetic link, no reason to suspect Dad may have had another family. But after reviewing property records and other public records, he discovered Ryan and Mia were from Dull originally, but then moved to Ithaca and lived there for a few years when they were young. Ithaca is only a few hours from my family home in Whitby. At some point, they moved back to Dull.

Is Ithaca where the connection started? But how and why? I have so many questions and no answers. Not yet.

I make my way back down the hall, through the living room, and into the galley-style kitchen. My eyes trail over the appliances. What can I break that would require a call to the landlord but not be too hard to fix?

I pull the oven out a few inches. It's a tight squeeze between the beige granite countertops. It takes a bit of wiggling, but eventually, I get it back far enough to fit my arm behind it. I reach down and yank on the plug, then push the oven back into place.

That should do it.

Chapter Three

RYAN

"He showed up here with your wallet and expected what, exactly? A blow job on your porch? In exchange for a shitty lunch at the Dull Diner and basic human decency?" Bernie waves a hand in the air, her dark, curly hair bouncing along with her emphatic movements.

I carefully flip the pancake in the skillet in front of me. "I paid for his lunch."

She props her hip on the edge of the counter. "What a prince. I am going to kill Austin."

"It's not his fault. He said they've only worked together for a few weeks. I'm sure he's great at work."

When he doesn't have to interact with women or children or, you know, people in general.

Austin is Bernie's older brother by five years. Bernie

and I have been best friends since preschool. We were inseparable up until middle school, when Mia's condition worsened and we moved to New York to be closer to hospitals that could handle the level of care she needed. Bernie and I stayed in touch though. Both of us were weirdos with boy names in a Podunk small town. Although Bernadette could have gone by her full name, she's always preferred Bernie.

She shakes her head. "You should have thrown those live crabs at him."

I snort. "If I had kept them, I would have. Maybe I should have let them live on the porch, like security dogs. Except crabs. Anyway, it doesn't matter. He came, he was annoying, then he saw Ari and freaked out and ran away screaming."

She snorts. "Screaming?"

"Internally, I'm sure. He was disgusted at the idea of dating someone who's," I glance toward the hall to make sure Ari isn't there, and lower my voice, " 'used goods.' "

Bernie's mouth pops open. "Are you fucking kidding me? He actually said that? I'm going to kill him. I'm going to find him and chop off his fucking nipples and make a belt out of them."

I tilt my head toward the bedrooms down the hall, where Ari is getting dressed. "Bernie. No f-words or Ed Gein references with juveniles in the home."

"Sorry, but he deserves it. Did you tell him she's even not your kid?"

I frown. "Of course not. She *is* my kid. Whether I

gave birth to her or not is irrelevant. And any so-called man who can't accept a child, any child, doesn't deserve my time."

Bernie picks up the coffee mug on the counter next to her and takes a sip. "You're right, of course. You're also a dickhead magnet and I don't know how to help you."

I chuckle and roll my eyes, carefully flipping another pancake. "I don't need help. I've only dated, like, four people in my whole life."

"Yeah. And they were all dicks. They could do studies on your ability to attract the dickiest of dicks. It's like a reverse superpower. When I told you I wanted to help you find you some dick, I was hoping for some non-dick dick." She sets her mug down with a clink.

Maybe she could find the guy from the grocery store.

"I think that little spiel deserves some kind of award for the most excessive use of the word dick in a single rant."

I'll probably never see the grocery store man again. He was definitely not a local. Probably just driving through and long gone at this point.

But seriously, is it too much to ask for someone, anyone, who isn't a total waste of space and also has above-average hygiene and a chiseled jawline?

I pour a couple of circles of batter onto the hot pan. "I forgot to tell you. We ran into Shane and *Samantha* at the store last night. She's pregnant."

Her mouth pops open. "Are you serious?"

"Yep."

"What a—"

I point the spatula in her direction. "If you say dick, I'm going to throw this at you."

She crosses her arms over her button-up black shirt. "So, you're telling me the antichrist has been conceived and I should brace for the upcoming apocalypse?"

I laugh. "Basically."

Footsteps thud down the hall. "Bernie!" Ari slams into her side, the braids I spent twenty minutes on this morning half undone already. If I try to tame the unruly strands, they will just revert to chaos within an hour. Ari cocks her head at Bernie. "What's a poco lips?"

Bernie reaches down, patting her head. "Nothing you need to worry about."

"Is my cape clean yet?" she asks me.

"It's in the dryer. It will be ready in a little bit."

She frowns. "I need it for my outfit."

I scan her hot-pink capri pants and blue-and-yellow-striped shirt.

"Yep. A red cape will look perfect." Bernie chuckles.

"I know. Can I play outside?"

"After breakfast, and only if you stay in front of the house." I can keep an eye on her from the porch while I get some work done. Our cul-de-sac contains four condos and two small homes, all of which are currently occupied, but not much traffic turns down our road. I just have to make sure she doesn't venture out to the busier cross street.

She scrambles into the seat at the round dining table.

I scoop the rest of the pancakes off the griddle and put together a plate, setting it in front of her.

"Did you want some food before you leave?" I ask Bernie, gesturing to the remaining stack.

"No thanks, I gotta get to work. I'll see you both Wednesday?"

"We'll be there."

"Bye, Bernie." Ari waves with her fork. "Tell Grandma hi and I love her."

"I will, sweetie."

Bernie works in IT at the hospital. Mom lives on the skilled nursing floor. She's been there for almost a year. I visit two to three times a week, sometimes with Ari and sometimes without, either on my lunch break or after work, whenever I can squeeze in some free time.

After Bernie leaves, we eat a quick breakfast. Afterward, I clean up and follow Ari outside, sitting on the porch with my laptop while she draws on the sidewalk with her chalk.

I check the messages for the rentals, replying to two inquiries on upcoming availability before opening the last one. The subject line reads: *Kitchen Conundrum.*

Hi,

The stove in unit 2E has developed a sudden aversion to

cooking. Nothing will turn on, and I've tried all the burners and the oven.

Any chance someone can come take a look? I'd appreciate it, and my stomach would too.

Desperately trying to not live off microwavable meals and junk food,

Jake in 2E

I pull up the rental contract. Jacob Fox. He's here for three weeks. No other occupants are listed.

Normally, I would put this in for Priscilla, but he's right across the street, and it's Saturday and I know she had some errands she wanted to get done today. I type out a quick message, asking him to let me know what time would be best for me to come over and check it out. Some renters don't want to interact, so I could go over there and fix it while he's out.

A couple of hours pass in a blur of phone calls, checking the website for new reservations, reconciling the account ledger, finalizing payroll for the next pay period, dealing with an issue with our payroll provider software—which means sitting on hold for forty-five minutes—and a million other little things. It's a lot, but all in all, it's not a bad gig. I get reduced rent in exchange for my services, and a decent paycheck.

Not enough to pay for Mom's hospice care when the trust runs dry, but that's a worry for another day.

I log back into the message portal. 2E has replied that I can come check it out anytime after ten.

It's ten thirty. Perfect. Best to get it over with. After plugging in the laptop to recharge, I grab the master key ring from the lockbox in my office.

"I'm just going to be across the street," I tell Ari when I reach the sidewalk where she's tracing something in pink chalk. "Stay here. I'll just be a few minutes." I tilt my head, eyeing her artwork. "Erm, tell me about your drawing there, baby?" It's long and phallic shaped with two giant circles at one end.

"It's a crocodile. His name's Jeff. He has big eyes."

I press my lips together and contemplate Jeff very seriously. "He looks great." I give her a thumbs-up before jogging across the street.

After knocking on the door, I turn and scan for Ari again. Past her, Mr. Enbom is outside on his patio, watering plants. A middle-aged divorcé and long-term renter, he lives in the house at the end of the street.

Mrs. Brennan's orange tabby cat sits in the window in the unit across from his, tail twitching behind him while he silently monitors the robins in the trees.

"Just a sec," a masculine voice calls from inside a few seconds before the door swings open.

I'm momentarily stunned into open-mouthed speechlessness by a brief glimpse of abs—*holy hell*—and a lean torso, and then a shirt drops, covering the exposed flesh. Well, some of the flesh. He's wearing a . . . is that a raccoon on his crop top?

"Hey. It's you." He flashes a grin.

My eyes lift to his face and my mouth falls open. "Oh."

It's the hottie from the grocery store.

He tugs at the shirt, frowning down at his midsection. "Uh, sorry about this. I grabbed the wrong top."

"I don't mind." The words pop out before I can stop them. Heat rushes to my face. I really need a filter between my brain and my mouth. He's wearing a woman's shirt. It's probably his girlfriend's.

He, thankfully, ignores my words. "If you tracked me down to pay me back, you really don't need to worry about it."

"No, it's not that." Although now that I know where he's staying, I really should find a way to pay him back. And I should stop staring at his exposed midriff.

Eyes up, Green.

He winces and gives up trying to cover his stomach. "Sorry about," he moves his hand in a circle in front of his chest, "all of this. I'll just, uh, fix myself. Come on in."

He moves back, heading down the hall toward the bedrooms.

I take a step just inside the front door, glancing down at the paperwork in my hand. "Is someone else staying here?" In the front room, there's a stack of letters on the desk and a black sweater draped over the chair. I don't hear anyone else moving or talking.

"No. Why?" He emerges from the hall, tugging a navy-blue T-shirt over his head, giving me another glimpse of his leanly muscled chest and trim waistline before he's covered.

Completely this time.

Pity.

"Well, the shirt, it was, I mean, it had a bedazzled raccoon on it." I lift the contract up. "Your application for the rental said there would be only one guest. It's not that big of a deal, I just need to record who's in residence for liability reasons."

"Application for the rental." His eyes narrow on the papers in my hand. "Why do you have my rental application?"

"You are Jacob Fox, right?"

"Yes. And you are . . ."

Confusion ripples through me, followed swiftly by realization. I haven't told him why I'm here yet. "I'm here because of your message about the stove."

He blinks. "What message?"

I frown. "You said the stove isn't turning on."

"Oh yeah, I thought I sent the message to the property manager. Ryan?"

I sigh and give him a weak smile. I get this all the time. "That's me. I'm Ryan."

Chapter Four

JAKE

Ryan is a woman. She's talking. She must be. Her mouth is moving, and I'm sure sounds are emerging, but my head is buzzing and I can't register any of it.

Ryan's a woman.

An extremely attractive, funny, kind-to-small-children-and-animals—probably, she doesn't look like she'd want to kick a puppy—woman.

What if we're related?

My entire being tenses in revolt, gaze scanning over her features, searching for a possible connection. She has blue eyes.

Really vividly pretty blue eyes, actually.

All my family, myself included, have dark eyes, like Dad. The brightness of her eyes is offset by short dark hair that curls slightly around her ears and brushes the delicate skin of her neck.

Brown hair is a trait we share, but a lot of people have dark hair, right? I'm sure most of the world.

Her features are petite. She has a button nose and a gently sloped jawline framing a wide mouth—definitely not like anyone in my family with our more striking features, bold chins, and patrician noses.

We cannot be related.

She's still talking, probably filling the void created by the gaping silence since I'm staring at her with my mouth hanging open like I've just had oral surgery and everything below my nose is numb.

"My parents thought I was going to be a boy and my grandfather is named Ryan, so that's what they planned on. Even though I obviously turned out to be a girl, they kept the name anyway. Don't get me wrong, I love it. But, yeah, it can cause confusion sometimes." She tucks a loose strand of hair behind her ear, chuckling awkwardly.

I rein in my scattered thoughts long enough to toss out some trite words. "It's a great name, Ryan. I like it."

Lame. The lamest. *Pull yourself together, man!* It doesn't matter that Ryan is a woman. This changes nothing. I still have a mystery to solve.

And it can all end here, once I open my mouth and ask Ryan why she was exchanging letters with my dad and why those letters revolved around Mia, Ryan's little sister.

Except, now that she's standing right in front of me, the words aren't coming.

How would I react if some stranger showed up, demanding answers about something that involved *my* departed sister? Not too friendly, and not ready to roll over and give up info, I imagine.

She jerks her thumb toward the kitchen. "Shall I check out the stove?"

"Yes. Right."

She heads through the house, and I follow her.

"Do you want some water or something?" I open the fridge and pull out a plastic bottle. If she drinks from this, I can send it in for DNA testing.

"No. Thanks."

I twist off the cap and take a drink. "Are you sure? I got plenty of bottles. They're nice and cold and refreshing."

She shoots me a confused look, her brows dipping.

Yep. I'm making it weird. There goes that idea.

She stands in front of the stove, pushing buttons, turning knobs, and of course nothing happens.

Would it be weird to offer to brush her hair?

How long will it take for her to figure out the issue? This same scenario happened to me at one of the cabins on my family's rental property before we turned it into a camp. It took me a good thirty minutes to realize it was simply unplugged. I have no idea why the tenants decided to do it, it's not like it's easy to pull the appliance out from the wall and tug the cord out, then push it all back in, but people do weird things.

She twists around to look at me. "Can you help me get this out from the wall?"

"Of course." Damn. She's quicker than I was. Maybe it's not surprising, since I was more than likely hungover at the time.

I stand next to her, wrapping my fingers around the back of the oven and tugging it forward on the right side while she mimics me on the left.

It's a heavy, stainless-steel oven, so the motion is ungainly and at one point my hip brushes hers.

"Sorry," I murmur.

"No problem. So," she grunts as we get it out from the wall a few inches, then she pulls her phone from her back pocket and turns on the flashlight. "Where are you visiting from?"

After a second's hesitation, I tell her the truth, if only to see her reaction. "I'm from Whitby. It's in New York."

She points the phone back behind the oven, peering down the back of it, and frowns. "Whitby? Never heard of it. I lived in Ithaca during high school and college. Though I didn't have a chance to explore the rest of the state much."

She didn't even flinch. She's either an Oscar-worthy actress, or she's truly never heard of Whitby. Ithaca is only a couple of hours away, but Whitby is tiny. Confusion pokes at me, questions popping up in my mind like an unwieldy jack in the box. There were never return addresses on the envelopes the letters were in. A printed label adorned the front of each one with our home address. Is it possible she isn't the letter writer? There can't be another Ryan and Mia in Dull. "It's a really small town, near the Catskills."

She sighs. "It's unplugged. I should have known those renters would do more than leave their crabs behind."

"Crabs?"

She waves a hand. "It's nothing. People are weird. So, is Whitby smaller than Dull?"

"Yep."

She pulls back and grips the side of the oven again. "We have to pull this out farther to get the plug back in the wall."

I help her wiggle the appliance farther and then she hoists herself up on the counter, lying on her belly to reach behind it.

The position showcases her trim waist, the subtle arch of her hip, and the curve of her ass in her tight jeans.

Lust blows through my body. My groin tightens.

Not the time. Not to mention the question of her paternity.

And with that thought, the lust exits as quickly as it rushed in, leaving me lightheaded.

I clear my throat. "Do you want me to do that? My arms are longer."

"I got it."

I keep my eyes focused on the corner of the stove while she finishes plugging it in and hops off the counter, wiping her hands on her pants. "That should do it." She turns one of the knobs, and the red light on the cooktop lights up. "There it is." She grins at me, the motion lighting up her whole face.

My heart stutters in my chest.

Literally, the organ shivers and then resumes beating like she just reached inside my ribcage and squeezed with the strength of her smile alone. What the ever-loving hell is going on?

"Uh, great. Thank you so much." I move toward the door, not wanting to prolong this conversation for a minute longer because I really want to extend it as long as I can.

"No problem." She blinks in surprise, following behind me. "Just send a message if you have any other issues."

"Absolutely." I open the front door and plaster a smile on my face as she brushes past me. "Thanks so much."

She waves and jogs down the porch steps.

I shut the door and lean back against it. I cannot even consider being mildly attracted to this woman until I know more. It's not like I can control it, but damn, if we're related, that's gross. Maybe only Mia was related?

There is no way to get Mia's DNA, since she's passed, but I have a plan to access her medical records if needed.

I groan and rub my head. How am I going to get Ryan's DNA now? I still have options. She does live right across the street.

I have visions of sneaking around at night in a trench coat with a fake mustache and bowler hat.

That might be my best option.

My phone dings and I slide it from my pocket. It's an email from Elaine, the business manager at the hospital, welcoming me to the team and outlining where to show up tomorrow, a reminder of the documents I need to bring, and some attachments to review.

I can't believe I'm doing this.

The information Dwayne obtained included where Mia worked before she died. She was a patient representative at the local hospital. I looked up the place online, checking job openings for months, and the minute there was an open maintenance position, I applied, had a phone interview with Elaine, and got the job.

Is this whole idea bananas? I moved to a new town—temporarily, sure—but clear across the country, obtained a job specifically where Mia used to work, and rented a unit specifically because Ryan manages it.

I move to the window, peering through the blinds.

Ryan is crouched down, talking to her daughter on the sidewalk. The little girl has chalk smudges all over her hands and smeared on her face.

I scan the side yard and driveway, and then arrive at the perfect plan.

Eureka.

Two garbage cans rest on the side of the house, one so full the top is propped up.

I truly am a trash panda.

Chapter Five

RYAN

"Hey, Ryan. Can I talk to you for a minute?"

We only made it two steps past Elaine's office door.

I spin around. "Of course, Elaine." My stomach twists.

I've been waiting for her to ask for a conversation with me. The bill for mom's care is over a month past due.

"Ari, you go on with Bernie. I'll be right there."

Bernie is waiting down the hall, outside of Mom's room. Ari runs ahead, her pink sneakers squeaking on the shiny blue linoleum.

Bernie gives me a commiserating wince before they disappear around the corner, heading to mom's room.

I follow Elaine into her office, and she shuts the door behind us.

Crap.

She moves behind her desk, motioning for me to take a seat.

I sit in the guest chair across from her, clutching my purse in my lap, staring at the stacks of papers lined up along one edge.

Her phone, computer, and keyboard are all aligned. Her dark hair is threaded through with gray and pulled back into a neat bun. Her blue pant suit is pressed and pristine—not so much as a ball of lint to mar the surface.

I'm wearing paint-stained overalls and I haven't shaved my legs in a week.

She gives me a sympathetic smile. "I'm sure you know why I needed to speak with you."

"I'm so sorry. I know the payment is late, but I'm still dealing with the trust stuff. They needed to do an accounting and the court has to review it, and they had all these delays and . . . I swear I'm going to have it to you as soon as I can."

She reaches across the desk to pat my hand. "I know, sweetie."

The trust is nearly depleted, but I don't want to tell her that. There's just enough in there to make Mom ineligible for any public benefits, but not enough to cover her hospital bills for the next few months.

"You know we will keep your Mom here, no matter

what. We would never turn her out when she needs twenty-four-hour medical care."

But.

She doesn't say the word. It's in her kind eyes, down-turned lips, and tight shoulders.

If I don't pay, they will send me to collections, eventually. We'll reach a point where they won't have a choice.

"I spoke with our billing department and got them to put a thirty-day hold on sending anything out in the mail, so that should buy you some time."

I nod. They send out three delinquency notices every thirty days before they take any action to refer to collections or their legal department. "Thank you. I really appreciate it."

"Of course. We miss Mia around here every day. You know we will do everything we can to help."

My temples throb with the beginning of a headache.

Life isn't hard enough as a single mom of a rambunctious child. I also have an aging parent with dementia and kidney disease who requires constant care.

After Dad died, his life insurance money was put into a trust, but when Mom's health declined, we had to draw from it.

"Here's the number to the Aging and Disability Resource Connection." She slides a business card across the desk. "They might be able to help. It's worth a shot."

I pick up the card and slip it in my purse. "Right.

Thanks, Elaine. I appreciate everything you've done for us."

She means well, but I've already tried everything.

They have a limit on how many people they can assist in hospice care—budget issues and whatnot—and they've met their maximum for the year. Someone literally has to die for Mom to move up on the list.

I exit Elaine's office, shutting the door behind me, and then move over to the wall, leaning back against it and taking a deep breath. I hold it for a few seconds before blowing it out, attempting to relax my tight shoulders.

My eyes fall shut. It's no good. I'm so stressed out that tension is seeping out of my pores at this point.

I have to pull it together. I can't let Ari see me all frazzled. I count, breathing in for eight and then releasing out for eight while thinking of everything I have to be grateful for. We have a place to live. I have a beautiful, healthy, smart little girl. I can put food on the table and clothes on our backs.

Yes, my mother is in hospice. Yes, some days she doesn't remember my name or Ari's, or anything, and she lashes out and it's scary, but she has good days too. And there are good days ahead.

Please let today be a good day.

The anxiety is the worst on days I bring Ari. I don't want her to witness her grandma's erratic behaviors. That's not how I want Ari to remember her. The nursing staff is pretty good at warning us ahead of time, and I didn't get a call today, so it should be fine.

My skin prickles.

I blink my eyes open. To my left, where Mia's pictures are hanging on the wall, the weight of another presence breaks through my attempts at relaxation.

My breath hitches, heart stuttering in my chest. "Jake?"

"Hey, Ryan."

I blink a few times. What the hell is 2E doing staring at me in the hallway of the hospital?

"What are you—?" I take in his outfit, a navy-blue, long-sleeve button-up with the logo of the hospital stamped on the breast pocket, dark pants, and tan work boots.

"You work here?"

Why is this so weird? I'm so shocked by his sudden appearance I can barely think straight. I haven't seen him since Saturday, when I plugged in his oven. It's Wednesday now. His truck has been gone every morning and parked out front by the time Ari and I get home. He must work early. Not that I've been paying a lot of attention or anything.

"Yeah. I started Monday. I was just taking a break and," he nods toward the pictures on the wall in front of him, "checking out this memorial."

I step in his direction, stopping beside him to face the wall.

The assorted photos and messages are familiar. In the

center is an eight-by-ten of Mia in black and white, laughing. I took it six years ago on a trip to the coast when Mia was pregnant. Our last trip together. Her blond hair is blowing back in the wind. She has Ari's nose and Mom's lips. Surrounding the central photo are a circle of smaller framed artifacts, a photo of Mia with hospital staff, another of Mia with a long-term care patient, and a few framed cards with handwritten messages.

I vaguely remember someone asking if I wanted to sign it, but it was within a month of her death. I was at home with a newborn and a terrible boyfriend, barely holding on to my sanity. Ari was exhausting, but also the only thing that kept me together. She was a miracle. A little piece of Mia.

"How did she die?" His voice is a low rumble.

I never tell people she died giving birth, although it's true. The thought makes my hackles rise. I would never want Ari to think she was the cause of her birth mother's passing. "She had a congenital heart condition."

"How old was she?"

"Twenty-two."

He shoves his hands in his pockets, looking down at the floor. "I lost my sister too."

My head whips in his direction. "When?"

Down the hall, a nurse opens a door. I vaguely register the sounds of murmured voices and distant beeps, but my attention is more focused on the man beside me.

"Twelve years ago." He shakes his head, rubbing the back of his neck. "Wow, I can't believe how long it's been."

"How old was she?"

"Fifteen. We were twins."

Shit. Without thought, I reach out and grab his hand, squeezing his fingers. "I'm sorry," I murmur.

"I'm sorry too."

We stand there, both of us staring at Mia in silence. But it's not weird. What's weird is that it's not weird. It's completely normal to stand here, staring at my dead sister's image while holding the hand of some guy I barely know.

Maybe it's the odd comfort of his presence, maybe it's Mia's laughing eyes, maybe it's because he's lost a sister too, or maybe it's because I've been alone and shouldering so much weight for so long . . . Whatever the reason, my mouth opens and words pour out.

"It's been so hard since she died. Her death was the worst pain imaginable. But I couldn't let it affect me, let alone overwhelm me. I have a daughter to think about. Then Mom got sick and I couldn't take care of her alone. Her memory started to fail, her moods became erratic, she started lashing out, getting physical, and then she needed dialysis frequently. I had to admit her to the skilled nursing hospice care here and it's just been . . . it's been so much, and it never gets easier, only harder. I don't know how much longer I can do this."

The last words emerge on a breath like my frustrations have run out of steam right as my lungs have run out of air.

I shut my eyes. I can't believe I completely unloaded on this poor guy.

But then his fingers squeeze mine and my eyes fly open.

"After I lost my twin, my dad got sick."

I swallow, hard. Not sure if I should ask him to elaborate or wait for him to speak. Thankfully, I don't have to consider my options long.

"He had prostate cancer. I was his primary caregiver until the end. It was awful. But I had something to focus on other than . . . the loss. When he passed, I didn't do a great job coping with everything that had happened in my life. I turned to alcohol and used it to escape, to avoid dealing with my grief. Which meant my family had to pick up the pieces of all my mistakes. Life can be super shitty. But you're still here. You're present. You're taking good care of your daughter. You're stronger than you realize."

We turn toward each other at the same time, our eyes locking, as if the movements are choreographed.

I'm not even sure how to respond to this strange, surprising, and vulnerable conversation, but then something strikes me. "You're only staying in Dull for three weeks. But you got a job here? I didn't think they hired temps."

He clears his throat and pulls his hand from mine,

the intimate connection severed. "Um, I rented another place longer term that's cheaper."

"Where are you staying?"

He waves a hand. "I can't remember the address. It's in the west part of town."

"Oh." There are at least a dozen different rental properties and apartments on that side. I guess that makes sense.

"I've got to get back to work." Jake gives me a tight smile.

I frown at his back. That was weird.

Maybe he doesn't want to be seen slacking since he just started this job.

A hand touches my shoulder and I spin around. It's Bernie.

"Hey, they just brought your mom lunch and Ari wants to help her eat. She's having a good day."

Mom. Right. "Yeah, I'm coming."

Still a little discombobulated from the whole interaction, I follow Bernie down the hall and into Mom's room.

She's sitting up in bed and smiling. Her gray hair is cut short for ease of care, and she's wearing the pink flannel pajamas Ari picked out for her for Christmas.

Since she's a long-term resident, the room isn't as stale as a normal hospital room, even though it has all the same bells and whistles. The walls are a sterile white, and the floors are the same squeaky linoleum from the hall, but she has framed pictures of family on a side table, a soft throw blanket on the guest chair, and a tall lamp in the corner casting a golden glow, counteracting the frosty LED lights in the ceiling.

Some of the tension eases from my shoulders.

She's happy. It's a good day.

Ari is sitting on the edge of her bed by the fold-out tray, while next to her, Bernie carefully opens the pudding cup.

Mom beams at her. "My Mia. Such a pretty girl."

Ari glances at me and then smiles brightly at her grandmother.

We've had a lot of discussions about how Grandma is a little bit like Dori and has a hard time holding on to memories. How sometimes she gets scared because she can't remember and she might get angry. Ari has witnessed her agitation, but it's never been directed at her, and we remove her from the situation quickly when it happens.

The nurse, Nicole, pulls me to the side by the door, far enough away that we won't distract Mom while she eats, but close enough to intervene if needed.

"She's lost a little bit of weight, she's sleeping more often, and she's been having quite a bit of itchiness, bad enough that she's scratching until she's breaking the skin."

"What does it mean?"

She offers a sympathetic wince. "It could be symptomatic of the ESRD progressing."

I nod. "Right." My stomach sinks.

"We've been treating it with hydrocortisone."

"Okay."

"I'll let you feed her lunch, and I'll be right down the hall if you need me."

"Thanks for the update." I squeeze her shoulder before she exits the room.

I move over to Mom's bedside, kissing the top of her head and breathing in the sharp, astringent scent of the hospital underlined with the strawberry shampoo we bring in for her. "Are we starting with chocolate pudding?"

"We should always start with dessert." Mom smiles up at me.

Ari's eyes widen. "Do you hear that, Momma? Always start with dessert."

I purse my lips. "How about sometimes start with dessert, like special occasions?"

She swirls the spoon in the pudding. "Like birthdays? My birthday is next week."

Mom swallows the bite of pudding Ari feeds her and then asks, "Are you having a big party?"

"Yes. And we'll come see you too," Ari assures her. "I'm sorry you can't come to the party."

Mom reaches out and cups her cheek with one hand. "My Mia. So sweet. And getting so big. Don't run around too much with your friends and overtire your heart, okay?"

"Okay." Ari feeds her another spoonful of pudding

before launching into a story about a field trip she went on with her summer camp.

Mom listens and eats, her eyes bright and interested.

It's a good day. A good moment.

Yes, my mom is dying, I owe the hospital more money than I can pay, and my life is mostly chaos, but at this moment, everything is okay enough. I can hold on to that.

Chapter Six

JAKE

"I know you think you need to do this alone, but you should call Finley. At the very least let her know you're okay," Dr. Dana says, her eyes narrowing at me, the shrewdness of her gaze slicing through me via video call even though she's on the other side of the country.

I sigh. Damn therapist, always calling me out on my shit and being all logical and reasonable. "I will. I left her a note, it's only been a week, and I talked to Oliver last weekend. He knows I'm okay. He won't let them freak out."

Well, he won't let Piper freak out. Finley though, who knows? He and Finley have a sort of love-hate relationship, even though they are business partners and very close to being in-laws.

"I still think you should have told them," she says.

"Noted."

She taps her pen on the pad of paper in her lap. "Have you talked to Ryan since you saw her at the hospital?"

"No." I shake my head. I only saw her from a distance when I got home from work last night. She was in her yard, playing with her daughter.

I've already explained the sheer panic that filled me when Ryan asked me about the job and the temporary rental earlier this week. I didn't think I would run into her at the hospital. I didn't know her mom was there.

Damn small towns. I should know better. It's a good thing I remembered all those apartments and condos lining the highway on the drive into town.

"The only thing I know for sure," since I received the DNA results yesterday, "is we aren't related."

Thankfully.

Dad didn't have a second family, at least not one he donated his chromosomes to. Of course, there was also the possibility of the connection being through Mom and not Dad. Mom took off when I was one and I never knew her, but that possibility has also been negated.

I ransacked Ryan's trash last Friday night, much to my internal shame and embarrassment. But I got what I needed, which was a bit of her hair. I grew up with five sisters. Their hair is everywhere. Plus Ryan has dark hair, and her daughter has blond hair, so it was easy enough to distinguish. Mailed it off on Saturday, paid for a rush job, and had the results by Thursday afternoon.

We aren't related. Not even distantly, like a fifth cousin or something. No links.

Along with the relief at not being related to Ryan came a whole lotta confusion. If we had been related, that might have given me some kind of answer. Now it's back to square one. Why? *Why why why*, the question that's been pounding in my head for months now.

Of course, it's still possible Mia was related to Dad somehow, and not Ryan. If she and Mia weren't full-blooded sisters, Ryan might not even know it. Maybe Dad donated to a sperm bank, and Ryan's mom was struggling to conceive. I mean, who knows, right? That would explain why Ryan's letters always had a lot of information about Mia and her life.

In the meantime, I've discovered a way to get more info on Mia. Medical info, anyway.

The admin staff at the hospital has been working on transferring old paper medical files into electronic versions. Everything is locked up in a room on the first floor, with all the file cabinets and scanning equipment.

The keys to the door are in Elaine's office, in the top drawer of her desk. I caught a glimpse of them when Elaine was telling me about the project yesterday. So now I just need to get into Elaine's office when she's not there and get ahold of those keys.

"The strangest part of the whole interaction was how I just opened up to her." It was the first time I volunteered information about what had happened to my twin to someone else.

"Why do you think you could broach the subject with Ryan?"

"I don't know. Maybe because she knows what it's like to lose a sister."

Her head tilts to one side. "Your sisters also lost a sister. And you're much closer to them. Plus, you all lost the same sister, even if the relationship dynamics weren't the same."

I frown. "I know." It's somehow different. Though Mia wasn't Ryan's twin. From what I've been able to figure out, Mia was about a year younger. "I'm not sure I understand it myself."

Maybe it's because we're closer in age. But that doesn't quite explain it either. Taylor is only a year older than me. Maybe it's because Ryan is a stranger. Maybe it's because she left me money in an envelope slid under the front door to repay me for the groceries. Maybe it's because there's something about her mere presence that prickles my skin and sends a ripple of warmth through my body.

Maybe it's because I haven't had sex in two years.

Her brows lift. "Do I get to be proud of you for journaling about Aria?"

I wince. "I'm trying."

Not trying at all. Actively avoiding.

What she's asking is impossible. It would be easier to

pluck the moon from the sky. Every time I try, my mind fixates on the last time I saw her.

Bloodied.

Broken.

My fault.

Bile rises in the back of my throat, along with the usual terror and guilt.

I push the bubbling emotions back down. I can't even say her name. How can I write down anything about her?

"Think about something that happened a long time ago, when you were little. Or something that involved your other siblings too. I'm sure you have plenty of material."

She's not wrong. With five sisters, I could pen a whole saga.

"You could even just write about her physical traits, what she looked like, an outfit you remember her wearing. Literally anything. When you're done, you can burn it. You don't have to share it with anyone, not even me. It's just for you."

"I know. I know it's important, and I'll try."

I never took the time to grieve. As a result, emotion tends to slap me in the face or crush me like an elephant sitting on my chest out of nowhere.

I need to deal with her death, confront it, not forget it, but move past it, otherwise the whole reason behind my drinking problem still exists. I don't necessarily *miss* alcohol.

What I miss is numbing the pain.

When the session is over and we sign off, I lean back and rub my face. Therapy is like running up a slippery hill on roller skates. Self-improvement is exhausting.

I grab a notebook from my bag, then go to the kitchen, pour a cup of coffee, and head out the front door.

Sitting on the wicker chair on the porch, I open the notebook and stare down at the empty page.

How the hell am I ever going to be able to do this?

A door slams across the street.

Ryan's little girl skips down the porch steps and grabs a scooter leaning against the fence, pushing it onto the sidewalk in front of her house.

"Hi." She grins at me, waving.

I lift my coffee mug in a salute and then take a sip before setting it on the blue mosaic table next to my chair.

She rides her scooter up and down the sidewalk, back and forth.

I drag my attention back to the page in front of me.

Focus.

The little girl is singing something softly, the sound barely audible.

It must be lonely, being an only child. It's not an existence I can imagine, being one of six, not to mention one part of two halves.

My bones ache with the loss.

Tires skid across pavement.

She's on the move, crossing the street to the walkway in front of my rental. "Do you know how to ride a bike?" she calls out. Her hair must have been clipped back at some point, but now the pink bow lists to one side, her curls waving around her head.

"Yeah."

"I can't." The words aren't remorseful, more direct. "Momma said I could have a bike maybe for my birthday. But I don't know how to ride it, so I don't know if it's really what I want."

"That's very pragmatic of you."

Her nose wrinkles. "What's prag-man-tic?"

Before I can correct her, or give her the definition, her head whips back toward her house, like a gazelle sensing a nearby predator.

The side door opens, and Ryan tosses a bag in the trash before the door slaps shut.

The little girl—I don't think I ever got her name—pushes away from my house, riding her scooter frantically back across the street.

I grin.

And a memory surfaces.

Aria and I were four, maybe five, and spent most of our days following Taylor around when she got home from school because she was a year older than us and Aria worshipped her. She was incredibly jealous of Taylor spending all day in first grade while we were stuck in part-time kindergarten.

Taylor had just had the training wheels removed

from her bicycle and was riding all over our property like she'd just been given the keys to the kingdom. Aria wanted desperately to learn to ride without training wheels. Taylor wouldn't let her tag along on her "baby bike."

So, while Taylor was in school, Aria stole her bike to teach herself. Except after attempting to ride it down the driveway, she went off the road and into the trees and popped a tire.

She was frantic. I helped her hide the evidence by taking the bike out to the far edges of the property and pushing it underneath an old, rusty, rundown tractor.

When Taylor came home and couldn't find her bike, she had a complete meltdown. She was convinced one of the guests had stolen it.

Aria was wracked with guilt over the whole thing.

I finally convinced her that we should go to Finley, who was around twelve at the time. She helped us fix the flat tire, and then we staged a whole scene with Aria and Taylor so that Aria could "find" the bike tucked into the trees near one of the rental cabins.

Taylor was so grateful, she spent the whole weekend with Aria, letting her tag along wherever she went.

Aria was so happy. Always so eager to please everyone around her. Family was more important to her than anything.

The ache in my chest deepens. Will the grief ever end? I loved her like there was no tomorrow, and then one day there wasn't.

"What are you drawing?"

Startled, I lift my gaze from the notebook page, locking eyes with the little girl on the sidewalk in front of the condo.

She's hanging on to my fence with one hand, her other hand on her scooter handle, while she rolls it back and forth with one leg.

I lift my pen. "I'm writing a story."

Her head tilts. "Is it about a superhero?"

The corners of my mouth tug upward, the hole in my chest suddenly less vast. "Sort of."

"I like Doctor Strange. He has a cool cape. I have a cape too." She gestures to her back.

"That's cool. I wish I had a cape."

She pushes the scooter up the walkway, coming a couple of feet closer. "Do you have a dog?"

"No."

Her lips press together. "What about a cat?"

"No."

She lets go of the scooter, letting it fall onto the grass as she walks up to the porch steps. "Hmm. My friend Bruce has a dog and a cat and a rabbit and three chickens. I don't have any pets either," she adds as if forgiving the offense.

"I do have sisters. They are like animals sometimes." I pick up my coffee and take a sip. It's barely lukewarm now.

She giggles. "Are they little or big?"

"Big. Well, not in size, but they are all older than me."

She hops up the steps and sits in the wicker seat next to me, swinging her legs. "I don't have any sisters or brothers."

"Do you want some?"

She shrugs. "Maybe. Momma says babies just cry and eat a lot and can't play or anything for *years*."

I chuckle. "I suppose that's true."

"I don't have a daddy." And then before I have a minute to absorb that nugget of info, she points at my legs. "What's on your pants?"

I glance down. "Those would be hot dogs." Archer gave them to me last Christmas. We have an ongoing debate because he is under the delusion that a hot dog meets the definition of a sandwich. He's a complete savage.

"I like hot dogs. And pizza. And chocolate cake."

"Me too."

"Why are you in your nighttime clothes?"

I shrug. "It's early. I'm lazy." I need more coffee. I pick up the mug and drink the rest of the brew.

"I don't have hot dog PJs, but I have rainbow ones. My momma doesn't wear pajamas."

I choke.

Holy shit.

Don't think about Ryan naked, don't think about Ryan naked, don't think about Ryan naked.

"She always sleeps in T-shirts and sweats."

I mop up my chin with my shirt and clear my throat a few times before asking the question burning the back of my throat. "So, uh, what happened to your daddy?"

She shrugs. "Not sure. Momma says she's my mom and my daddy, and I have Grandma and Bernie who said I have an aunt mommy which is way better than having even three daddies because men are always the problem and not the solution."

From all my interactions with Bernie at the hospital this week, that sounds exactly like something she would say.

"That's a fairly accurate assessment," I agree.

She nods solemnly.

Did she say "aunt mommy"? What does that mean?

Before I can ask any more probing questions to clarify, she sits up straighter, waving her little hand back and forth quickly. "Momma! I'm over here!"

Ryan is frowning at us from her front porch, hands on her hips. She's wearing cutoff shorts and an oversized white T-shirt with a giant red heart on the front.

Her face dark, she strides across the street.

The little voice beside me yanks my gaze from Ryan's rapid approach. "Are you coming to my party tomorrow?"

"Erm, I don't think so. I didn't get an invitation."

"Momma!" she calls out. "You have to bring an invitation to my party!"

"What's the party for?" I ask.

"It's my birthday."

"Happy birthday."

She wrinkles her nose. "It's not my birthday yet, but we had to have my party tomorrow."

"I would like to come, but we have to make sure it's okay with your mom first."

Ryan reaches the porch, her eyes flicking from me to her daughter. "Ari, you shouldn't be bothering Jake."

My heart drops down into my stomach.

This is the first time I've heard the little girl's name.

Did she say Ari?

I stare at Ryan, the name sinking into my consciousness, then look over at the small figure on my left, to her blue shoes kicking up and down, up and down.

Ari.

Not Aria. But damn, that's really close. What if it's short for Aria?

It might not be. It might mean nothing. There is this thing that I've experienced since my sister died, called frequency illusion. Her name is everywhere. From the lips of a woman talking to her daughter at the grocery store, to a character in a movie or book or TV show. When I was younger, I thought it was some kind of sign, like she was talking to me or sending me some kind of message. I know better now.

When something is on your mind, you'll notice it more in your environment. It doesn't mean it's suddenly more common, it's just that you're more aware of it. Like when you really want a Porsche 911 GT3 RS and then you see them everywhere. It's not that there are more Porsches driving about, it's that your focus makes you notice them when you otherwise wouldn't have.

But still.

The fact is, this woman who was exchanging letters with my father just happened to name her daughter something eerily similar to my twin. What are the odds? Then again, Ari could be short for Ariana or something.

Ari's eyes widen. "He's not a stranger. We talked to him at the store, and he's our neighbor, and he has hot dogs on his PJs."

"She's not bothering me. It's fine," I manage to get out, my voice raspier than intended. I lift my coffee cup to my lips. It's empty. I set it back down.

"So can you come to my party?" Ari asks.

Ryan speaks before I can so much as open my mouth. "He's probably busy this weekend. It's very last-minute."

"I'm not busy at all. I'd love to be there. That is, if it's okay with you?"

Chapter Seven

RYAN

Damn him and his politeness and his stupidly cute hot dog pajamas.

"Of course it's okay." I force brightness into my voice.

Great. Now I get to spend more time with the hot guy I verbally drowned with all my life's greatest disasters.

"What time does it start?" Jake's dark eyes lock with mine.

Heat fills my face. Why is he looking at me like that? Is there a screen on my forehead replaying every dirty thought I've had about him over the last week?

I can't tell him he's not invited. It would be rude, and Ari would be upset and ask *why* and I have no good reason other than the fact that I'm monumentally embarrassed.

Besides, there will be a lot of other people there. It's not like I'll have to talk to him the whole time. I will be busy running games and monitoring a gaggle of children.

He'll probably show up for a second and leave. He's new in town. He doesn't know anyone.

"It starts at four." To make it easier on the kids who still take afternoon naps. "Nothing fancy, some finger foods and cake and games and whatnot."

His penetrating gaze finally moves away, landing on Ari, still sitting in the seat next to him. "What do you want for your birthday?"

I lift my hands. "Oh, you don't have to—"

But Ari cuts me off. "I want nail polish, an iPhone, a necklace, a puppy, new bedtime storybooks, three cookies, and new paints because mine got all dried out."

"Three cookies?" He lifts a brow.

Ari nods emphatically.

I sigh. "I normally only let her have two."

He chuckles.

"Come on. We have to leave for camp in twenty minutes. Why don't you go grab your lunch and the toy you wanted to bring for share time? I have to talk to Jake for a second about work stuff."

Ari wrinkles her nose. "Fine."

She trudges back across the street, grabbing her scooter as she goes, moving as slowly as possible.

I make sure she's safely on the sidewalk in front of our house before I turn back. "You don't have to come."

His head cocks to one side. "I want to. She's a sweet kid. I'm always down for parties and cupcakes and games." He claps his hands together. "Now, what can I get her that you haven't already bought? Or maybe I can grab something that would help you both. Is she outgrowing any clothes? She's at the age where growth spurts happen overnight."

"That's too true. Do you have kids?"

"No, but my family runs a kids camp back in Whitby and I've spent a lot of time with the campers. They'll arrive on a Friday wearing pants that hit their shoes, and by the following week, their pants are above the ankle. It's kind of incredible."

I hate asking for anything, really, but this is Ari's birthday and I can swallow my pride for her to have some new clothes. I donated a bunch of her old summer clothes a couple of weeks ago because she's outgrown them.

"She could use some new shorts and T-shirts. She likes superheroes and anything in bright colors."

"Size?"

"Six or seven."

He nods. "Things to grow into. Got it. I'll see you both tomorrow then." His smile is easy and bright.

"Thanks." I start down the porch steps and then stop and turn back around. "I'm sorry about the other day."

He's on his feet, his hand halfway to the doorknob. His brows draw together in confusion.

I clear my throat. "The whole info dump all over you earlier this week. At the hospital. I didn't mean to make things weird or uncomfortable."

His face clears. "It's okay. Really. Sometimes you have to let out a little steam or else you'll get burned."

I nod, turning on my heel. "Thanks."

"I like weird," he says, the words so quiet I'm not sure I hear them correctly.

I spin around, but he's already inside, the door clicking shut softly behind him.

"Why did I let you have a cupcake before the party?" I mutter under my breath.

"Because you're a sucker." Ari's giant eyes are sparkling even as I'm swiping chocolate frosting off of her chin.

"We need to change your shirt."

Her hand lifts. "You know it will just get dirty again."

Smartass. "That might be true, but what about the green one?"

Her nose wrinkles. "I can't wear green to my party."

"Why not?"

"It's not a party color."

"Of course. I should have known."

I finish cleaning off her face and then assist in tugging

the dirty shirt up over her head. "Pick something. I have to set out snacks. Your friends will be here any minute." I take the shirt through the kitchen and into the laundry room, squirting it with stain remover and tossing it in the washer.

"Hey." Bernie's voice rings through the house. "I'm here and ready to help with whatever you need. And I brought more masks."

I meet her in the kitchen. "You are a goddess."

She bows while handing me the bag of superhero masks. "The goddess of children's parties all over the land. Now what do you need?"

We spend the next twenty minutes setting up the games in the backyard and filling one of the picnic tables with drinks and snacks.

The doorbell rings, then it rings again and again and time becomes a blur of greeting guests, showing them where to put presents, handing out the superhero masks, and general mayhem. Some parents stay to hang out, others drop and run, and by the time it's all said and done we've got a house full of ten hyper kids and almost the same number of parents.

It takes a little bit of maneuvering, but I eventually herd all the kids into the backyard around one of the picnic tables for the first game.

We've set up a row of paper cups filled with minia-ture superheroes frozen in ice. Next to the cups are brightly colored water guns, one per kid.

I clap my hands to get their attention. "The game is

called Superhero Rescue. Frozen inside each of these cups are two superhero figurines. We're going to cut the ice blocks out of the cups, and when I say go, you will use the water guns filled with warm water to melt the ice and rescue the heroes. If you run out of water, we've got a bucket where you can refill it over by the door. First team to free their figurine wins the prize. Are there any questions?"

Bruce, a dark-haired boy from Ari's school, shoots his hand in the air.

"Yes, Bruce?"

"Can we have cake first?" A line of chocolate is smeared over his chin.

"Bruce, honey, did you already have some cake?" his mom asks.

His eyes widen. "No."

I smother a laugh. "Just pick out your gun. We'll have cake soon, okay?"

There's a shuffling of squirt guns around the table and only a couple of slight disagreements over the purple one before all of the kids are ready.

"Ready, set, go!"

Laughter and anarchy ensue. Bruce screams like a banshee and squirts any and everything within his target range.

No more cake for Bruce.

"Try not to get your friends wet," I call out, but no one listens. No one is getting upset, yet, so I let it slide. I keep an eye on their progress for a minute, and then Bernie's laugh catches my attention.

She's sitting in one of the Adirondack chairs over by the unlit firepit, talking with Jake.

My stomach flips.

When did he get here? Bernie must've answered the door for him.

He says something and she reaches over, patting his arm.

My stomach twists.

They work together. I'm sure that's how they know each other and it doesn't matter anyway. It's fine. She can like him. She's single, childless, and awesome. It has nothing to do with me.

I wrench my gaze back to the game and focus on refereeing some of the kids with poor aim who keep hitting their friends with the water instead of the frozen superheroes.

Once the game is done, I make the executive decision to have food and cake now, so the kids can burn off some of the sugar with the rest of the activities.

Bernie helps me with cutting and distributing the cake, and we keep it all outside to help with the eventual cleanup.

When we've handed out the last slice, she nudges me with her elbow and angles her head toward mine. "You didn't tell me Donuts is your neighbor. You know he works at the hospital?"

"Donuts?"

"Jake. He brought donuts on his first day to try and kiss all our asses."

I chuckle. "Ah. Big mistake."

"Huge."

"I saw him at the hospital when I was there last week. He's renting the house across the street."

No need to mention how he bought me groceries, the intensely personal conversation we had, or how I wanted to rip off his hot dog pajamas yesterday morning and have my wicked way with him.

"What do you think about him?" she asks.

I follow Bernie's gaze across the yard to where Jake is standing, eating cake and talking to Bruce's dad.

One of the kids walks up to them and says something, and Jake spreads his lips in a feral grin, exposing chocolate-covered teeth.

The kids around him bust up laughing.

"What do you mean what do I think about him? I barely know him." I bite my lip. "Except when we were talking at the hospital I sort of lost it and word-gurgitated all over him. About Mom, Mia, and . . ." I sigh. "I wordgitated on him." I guess I am going to mention that conversation. I've never withheld anything from Bernie, no matter how embarrassing.

She snorts out a laugh. "How did that go?"

"Surprisingly well. He didn't run away screaming or tell anyone else about it, if you haven't heard anything so . . . there's that."

"Yeah. He's pretty cool. I was thinking about asking him out."

My gaze snaps back to her profile. My entire body clenches in horror at the image of Bernie with Jake.

But that's not fair.

"You should go for it. He seems nice." I push the words out, struggling to remain nonchalant.

Bernie laughs. "Relax, I was messing with you. I'll stay off your territory."

My face heats and the tension in my body ratchets up a notch. "He's not my territory. You can do what you want with him."

She rolls her eyes. "Oh, please. You always do this thing where you act like you don't like someone, but then your shoulders are up by your ears," she motions to me, "and you look ridiculous."

I force my shoulders to relax. "I don't do that."

"Uh, yeah you do. It's obvious you have a thing for him."

Dammit. I don't even know him, but I do like him. At least the looks of him. I don't want to like him. I don't want to get close just to discover he's terrible in some way. And that will be the inevitable end. It's so much better when you can build someone up in your mind and not find out their imperfections.

"Obvious?" The thought is terrifying. "Why would you say that?"

"You looked over at him a minute ago and your pupils turned into hearts and pulsed outside your eyes like a cartoon character." She puts a hand on my shoulder before I can voice any kind of denial. "Don't worry, I can only tell because I know you so well. He's as oblivious to your tells as you are to his."

"What do you mean?"

"When you're not looking, he stares at you like Ari looks at her cape. Also, he's been asking around about you."

"He did? When?"

"At the hospital. I overheard him talking to—"

"Ryan, thanks for having us." Michelle rests a hand on my shoulder and squeezes. She lives a few blocks over and has a five-year-old daughter. "We have a family obligation to get to. But Ari is still coming over next weekend for a sleepover, right?"

"She'll be there." We take turns having the girls over, alternating every month, giving Michelle and her husband a chance for a date night and giving me a night without Ari, a night to work or clean or sit around wondering what the heck normal twenty-somethings do on a weekend night. We say goodbye, and I give her daughter, Angelica, a goodie bag before they leave.

After everyone finishes cake, we go through a few more outdoor activities: a ball toss, pin the cape on the superhero, and a spiñata—the less violent version of a piñata. Then the whole group heads inside and fills the living room while Ari opens presents on the couch, oohing and ahhing over each and every one, hugging every person who brought her a gift, which makes it take twice as long but I'm not going to stop her.

The entire time, Jake is a palpable presence, hovering at the edges of the room and making small talk with the other parents.

After the presents are all opened, things start winding down. I chat with everyone I can while people continue to snack on the finger foods set out. People trickle their way out the door. Before I know it, I'm saying goodbye to the last of the guests, and it's only Ari and me and the house is quiet and getting darker by the minute.

When did Jake leave? He must have snuck out when I was helping Bernie take some of the leftover cake to her car so she could bring it to the hospital in the morning to share with the staff. He didn't say goodbye.

It doesn't matter.

I eyeball the living room. It's not *too* much of a mess. My eyes trail over some wrapping paper crumpled up on the floor and ribbon strewn over the side of the couch arm.

The backyard is another matter entirely, not to mention the kitchen. I should get the snacks put away and a load of dishes in at the very least. I won't be able to sleep until it's somewhat tidied up, and Ari still needs to take a bath.

"Ari?" I call out. Where is she? I glance down the hall, but the bathroom and bedrooms are dark. The backyard light is still on though.

I push open the door.

"If you make this one, I'll stand on my head and crow like a rooster."

Ari's laughter echoes through the night air.

Jake is holding up a big black garbage bag, stretched open. About ten feet away, Ari is holding an empty soda can. She chucks it toward him, and he shifts the bag so that the can lands inside.

"She shoots, she scores!"

Ari claps and yells, laughing. "Now you have to stand on your head and crow."

He didn't leave. He's cleaning up the mess, and he roped Ari into it by turning it into a game.

Shit.

He might actually be perfect.

Chapter Eight

JAKE

"Fruit punch?"

"Sounds great. Thanks."

Ryan hands me the juice box before settling in the Adirondack chair beside me. "Sorry, I don't have anything more adult-ish."

"I don't drink, so it's perfect."

Her head tilts. "You mentioned that the other day. You used alcohol to avoid dealing with everything."

"More or less." I avert my gaze to the flickering flames in the firepit in front of us. "It took me longer than I care to admit that I can't have even one drink without it turning into drinking to excess. It's easier to keep a tiger in a cage than on a leash."

Why am I always talking to Ryan about things better kept on the inside? I take a long draw on my juice.

I'm honestly not even sure exactly how I ended up here, sitting around the firepit in Ryan and Ari's backyard alone with Ryan.

After I helped them clean up the backyard, I offered to help with the kitchen and dishes while Ari got ready for bed.

I couldn't help but listen in to some of the bedtime routine, which included singing off-key Taylor Swift songs in the bathtub and Ryan reading to Ari in all kinds of funny voices. Then Ari delaying bedtime by asking for a glass of water and needing to use the bathroom at least three times before it was finally over.

She's a good mom. An *aunt mom*, according to Ari. I definitely want more information on that. Where's Ari's dad?

"Thank you for helping with all the cleanup. And for Ari's gifts."

I managed to grab her some clothes and then stumbled across a book, *The Velveteen Rabbit*, in the toy section. It came with a plush rabbit. I shouldn't have grabbed it. I almost didn't. But it was one of Aria's favorites. She'd even had the same Velveteen Rabbit stuffed animal. Without even meaning to, my hand reached for it and tucked it under my arm with the other items. I just had to get it.

"It's not a problem at all. I'm sure you're exhausted, and I truly have nothing else going on. My big plans tonight would have involved sitting on my porch alone. At least now I have good company."

I lift the juice box in her direction, and she taps her own against it with a laugh.

She settles back in the seat, taking a deep breath and shutting her eyes while the flames dance in a honeyed glow over her features.

Her dark hair has been scraped back into a short ponytail. She washed her face and changed into sweats while she was getting Ari ready for bed. She must be exhausted. And yet attraction sizzles in the air between us, like a rope I could reach out and tug on.

We sit in silence for a minute, while fire crackles and the wind rustles in the leaves overhead.

I almost don't want to ruin it. But this is also an opportunity to get some answers to questions that have been plaguing me since my conversation with Ari yesterday morning.

"It was a good party."

She opens her eyes, her head rolling toward me. "It was great. I am so glad it's over."

"It's got to be hard, doing all of this yourself."

One shoulder shrugs. "I have Bernie. And you helped me clean up so not too much work at all." Her gaze narrows. "Was that your sneaky way of asking where Ari's father is?"

The corner of my mouth tugs up. "Partially. I was curious because Ari mentioned something yesterday about you being *aunt* mommy?"

She nods once. "Right. Ari is technically my niece. Mia was Ari's mom."

The pieces realign in my head. Ari just turned six, and on the memorial in the hospital, Mia died almost six years ago. Wait— "She died giving birth to Ari?"

She winces, glancing toward the back door. "Yes, but it was because of her heart condition. She knew the risks when she found out she was pregnant. But she wanted Ari more than anything in this world. No one could convince her otherwise."

"The dad didn't want to be involved?"

She sighs, her head leaning back against the back of the chair. "Mia never said who he was. She went to some conference for the hospital and hooked up with someone. It was a one-night stand. I think he was a doctor or something, maybe even married. She would just say he wasn't available."

"Have you ever thought about trying to find him?"

Her brows dip. "It might be bad of me, but I don't really want to know. What if he wants to take her? I couldn't handle that. And maybe it would ruin his life, if he's married. He doesn't live here, I know that much, and I couldn't bear to part with her. Is that wrong?"

I shake my head. "No. You're doing the best you can."

She gives a half shrug. "Maybe when she gets old enough, I'll let her decide. We can do one of those genetic match sites or whatever. I just, I have enough right now on my plate, and losing Mia was the hardest thing I've ever had to go through. I couldn't handle losing Ari too. But you understand. You lost a sister. How did she pass? If you don't mind me asking?"

I swallow. I never talk about it. My chest gets tight and heavy, throat closing up. But somehow the words push their way through. "It was a car accident."

She winces.

And then even though my trachea is probably a pinpoint, the words keep coming.

"We were in the car together when it happened."

There's a long pause. I stare up at the night sky, focusing on a wispy cloud passing over the moon, unable to bring myself to look at her.

"Well, fuck," she says.

A surprised laugh barks out of me. I turn my head to meet her gaze. "That might be the most appropriate response ever."

She groans, slamming her juice box on the small table between us. "Death is fucking stupid. I have to say it sometimes. It's the worst. It's impossible to fathom that someone who means so much can just be gone. Forever. Someone said to me once that grief is love with nowhere to go. I know you can't have one without the other, but it fucking hurts. It sucks."

Truer words have never been spoken. "It really does suck." My fingers drum on the arm rest. "After the car accident, it was a rough few years. My dad never quite recovered from the loss."

"And then you took care of him when he had cancer."

I nod.

"You said you had other family too?"

"Sisters. Four of them."

Her brows lift. "Wow, four sisters? Are they older or younger?"

"All older than me. Finley, Mindy, Piper, and Taylor. Finley is the eldest. She raised the rest of us. Our mom took off when I was one. Finley was eight at the time. After Dad died, she ran our family property singlehandedly. I helped, but I was mostly a burden."

"I'm sure that's not true."

I hold up a hand. "Oh, it's very true. I was coping with everything that had happened by swimming to the bottom of every bottle I could find. And it's like they say, first you take a drink and then the drink takes you. We almost lost the property."

"I'm sure that was due to more than just you."

I dip my head in acknowledgment. "That's true, but I didn't help. We were struggling to keep it afloat. We had a bunch of cabin rentals, kind of like you have going on here, but in the woods. They were old and outdated and falling apart. Then some of the nearby ski resorts upgraded and we had almost nothing to offer paying customers in comparison. Finley refused to let it go, even when we were up to our eyeballs in debt. Then this completely ridiculous New York City billionaire pressured her to sell and offered a boatload of cash."

"You're smiling. There's definitely a story there. You told me your family runs a kids' camp or something?"

I nod. "Yeah. The ridiculous billionaire, his name's Oliver Nichols, and he's a giant pain in my ass." A giant pain that is likely even now getting ready to send in some of his henchmen to locate me. "Oliver and Finley eventually negotiated a joint-ownership agreement for the land and converted it to the camp. Finley manages the camp, and Oliver provides the funding. And he's going to marry my other sister, Piper."

"Wait." She straightens in her seat. "Piper? Piper Fox? The artist? Your sister is Piper Fox?"

"Yep."

Her mouth drops open. "Stop it. No way! I've seen some of her work. It's incredible. She did an installation for the school of medicine at Ithaca. It was a miniature bronze sculpture, with two figures, and one had broken off a piece of their heart and was sticking it in the other one's chest. It sounds weird and gross, but it was really cool. It was representative of the pieces of ourselves we give up helping others. I've never forgotten it. Is all your family living in New York?"

"All except Mindy. She's on the road right now with her boyfriend, Luke Fletcher. She owns a record label, so she stays pretty busy."

She lifts a hand up, her palm flat in a stopping motion. "Okay, hold on. I've heard of Luke Fletcher and Mindy Fox. You have a lot of famous sisters."

"They are incredible. But don't ever tell them I said so."

She angles her legs toward me. "If your whole family is all there, why did you leave? And come to Dull, of all places?"

I don't want to lie to her. But how can I tell her the truth? *I came looking for you.* I can't tell her. Not yet. But I can give her a partial truth. "I've lived there my whole life. I've never left except for vacations. I needed to experience something new, have a change of scenery. You said you lived in Ithaca. Why did you leave to move here?"

"I moved back home after Mia got pregnant."

I prop my elbow on the armrest, leaning closer. "That had to be hard. You said you lived in Ithaca since middle school and so you were, what, early twenties when Mia was pregnant?"

"Yeah. I had just finished college. I had planned on going into a nursing program in the fall at Cornell. I received my acceptance letter right before Ari was born and Mia died."

"Well, fuck."

She chuckles and points at me. "Yep. There it is again."

"Appropriate in all kinds of fuckworthy situations."

"So many of those in my life," she murmurs and then pushes to her feet. "Did you want more juice?"

I stand and take a step toward her, the space between us shrinking to inches. "Thanks, but I better not. Too much sugar and I'll be taking everyone out with me like Bruce."

She grins. "He was a little intense."

"You only think that because you haven't seen me after two juice boxes."

Her head tips back and she laughs.

Euphoria fills me. I did that, I made her laugh. I caused this smile she's giving me, the one that reaches her eyes and fills her face with a light that can't be explained by the flickering glow of the fire.

Our eyes lock.

My gaze dips to her mouth.

Need spears through me, a stab in the gut that shoots straight down to my cock.

Fuck, indeed.

Her smile falters, and she shifts on the uneven stones beneath our feet, stumbling. I reach out to steady her, grabbing her shoulders.

She looks up into my face. "Thank you."

"Momma?"

We leap away from each other so quickly I almost topple over the chair behind me.

Ari stands in the open doorway, rubbing her eyes. "I'm thirsty."

Ryan spins away, immediately moving into parent mode and heading toward Ari. "You can have one small sip of water and then back to bed."

"But I want to stay up and watch the fire too."

"Not tonight."

"Why?"

"It's been a really long day."

"But Momma!"

"Aria Marie Green . . ." she says as they disappear inside the house and their voices fade into indecipherable sounds.

So. I guess Ari *is* short for Aria.

Fuck.

Chapter Nine

RYAN

"She's having an off day." Bernie offers me a sympathetic wince before winding her arm through mine as we walk toward Mom's room.

"I'm glad Ari didn't come with me then." It's one of her summer camp days. Normally she loves going, but she was extra clingy today.

I couldn't bring her with me though. For one, I already paid for the day camp. For two, it was only a half day anyway. Also, I wanted to see Mom without having to worry if Ari would witness a bad day.

"The light in the bathroom is out so Jake might be in there replacing it. He's almost done though."

Jake.

Damn.

I haven't seen him since Ari's party on Saturday. I've been avoiding him. After Ari interrupted us the other night when we were having that charged sort of *moment*, he hightailed it out of there like he was being chased by a swarm of killer wasps.

Did he just get caught up, like I did, but then panicked and ran? Maybe he realized he was about to kiss a single mom with no money, no real future outside of Dull, Oregon, and chocolate cake stains on her shirt.

Maybe he wasn't going to kiss me at all. Did I misread the situation?

Possibly. It's been a while since I actually . . . liked someone enough to care.

He's been through so much. He's imperfect in a way that's so perfect. Which means I'm sure I'll find out something terrible about him.

Or he'll find something terrible about me.

I'm almost thirty, and other than raising an amazing child, I have nothing to show for my life.

I have a degree I can't use, a dying parent I can't take care of, and a vagina that hasn't had company in almost five years.

Pathetic.

"Did I tell you how I overheard him asking about you?"

"What? Oh, right." I had forgotten. She was going to tell me something at Ari's party. "What did he say?"

"He was asking Elaine about you, and Mia, and your

mom. Random stuff, totally digging for intel. I told you he's into you."

What kind of questions was he asking? Is that weird?

We reach Mom's door, and I can't ask her for more details, because Mom is agitated, her voice rising as I enter the room. "I don't know you. Where's Anderson? Why are you here? Are you trying to steal from me?"

My heart sinks. Anderson was my father.

"Hey, Mom." I stride over to her bedside and take her hand from where she's smacking her palm on the bed rail.

Her fingers clench around mine, her eyes pleading. "Ryan. Where is your father? It's almost dinner time. Is Mia playing outside? You need to make sure she doesn't run around too much."

"I'll grab the nurse to see if they can give her some meds," Bernie murmurs before disappearing out the door.

I swallow back the lump in my throat and sit in the seat beside her. "It's okay, Mom. I'll watch Mia. It's all going to be fine."

She reaches over and pats the top of my hand. "You're such a good sister. I don't know what we would do without you looking after our baby." She leans back in the bed and shuts her eyes.

This whole conversation is the story of my childhood. Most of my days revolved around making sure my baby sister Mia didn't overexert herself and send her heart into a tailspin, an impossible task when we were both young and wanting to play with all the other kids.

I resented it sometimes when I was assigned to watch Mia instead of being able to run around with my friends. Never outwardly. I shoved it down inside because Mia suffered enough with the forced inactivity, not to mention the innumerable doctor and hospital visits where she was poked and prodded and tested. I would give up a million summer days for one more hour with her.

"Are you okay?"

My head shoots up and I lock eyes with Jake, hovering outside the bathroom door, his concerned gaze fixed on me. "I'm fine."

I'm not fine.

My mom is dying, slowly. I'm exhausted.

His eyes search mine, brow creasing in concern. "If you need anything, anything at all . . . let me know." He disappears out the door.

I turn back to Mom.

Maybe I'm imagining things, seeing what I hope for every day, but her eyes are clear, and her gaze is direct. "You're doing a great job with Ari. Mia would be so pleased."

My mouth pops open. "Mom?" I whisper.

"Come here, baby." She uses one hand to scoot in her bed, making a space, and then opens her arms.

She's so frail, I don't want to hurt her, but I can't

pass up the opportunity to be held by my mom. Any time could be the last. I carefully slide in next to her, leaning lightly against her shoulder.

Her hand covers mine. "I know you miss Mia. I miss her too."

"I know." I shut my eyes.

For a minute, we just sit there. I commit the sensations to memory. The scent of her strawberry shampoo, her fragile arm brushing against mine, the sound of her breath moving in and out.

"Can you smell it?"

I open my eyes and tilt my head toward her. "Smell what?"

"Your father's cigar. He used to smoke one every time we brought home Mia from the hospital. Do you remember?"

"Yes." Sort of. I was five when he passed away.

She breathes in slowly, then out, and chuckles. "He tried to hide it from me. I used to get so angry with him." She's not mad now, humor wreathing her face. "I'll never forget that smell, tobacco, leather, and spices." Her nose wrinkles.

I smell nothing.

She sucks in a gasp, squeezing my hand. "Oh, she's here. I was hoping she would show up when you came to visit." She waves toward the corner of the room. "She never speaks. She just waves."

"Who does?" I follow her gaze. There's nothing

there, only a framed picture of a sailboat and an unused outlet on the wall.

Goose bumps prickle over my skin, the glow in her smile and focus in her gaze trapping me in the moment.

"It's Mia, of course."

My throat tightens. She *really* sees her.

Maybe she is hallucinating, but the air is charged, electric, the moment itself both spine-tingling and somehow sacred.

"She is always so beautiful. She looks exactly like she did when she was pregnant with Ari, all glowing." Her head tilts. "Who's your friend?" she calls out. Her lips purse and she points and then looks at me. "You see them? The other girl with her?"

I shake my head.

Her smile dims. "They're gone now. Don't worry, Mia will be back. She's been here every day. We'll see her again tomorrow." She's already settled back, her eyes closing.

Some of the nurses have told me stories about end-of-life visions, but I've never experienced it for myself. It's sort of eerie, and sort of awe-inspiring. I'm not sure what to think about any of it.

I'm emotionally drained by the time I step off the elevator into the lobby an hour later. I head for the front doors, then freeze. Shane and Samantha are walking in.

Panic floods through me. I can't deal with them right now.

I glance around.

I have nowhere to go.

Unless I go to the bathroom.

Keeping my head down, I cut to the left, walking fast, but not too quickly. Don't want to draw attention to myself.

I hold my breath until I've reached the recess in the wall where the restrooms are. Once I'm out of sight, I stop and peer back around the corner.

Shane and Samantha are standing in front of the elevator, holding hands, making quiet conversation.

Probably here to see the baby doctor.

They disappear onto the elevator, and I lean back, resting against the wall for a second and blowing out a breath. I'll just recover here for a second. Not moving sounds great. My mind plays the tape forward, contemplating everything that's still left in my day, picking up Ari, cleaning out a rental, dinner, bath time, cleaning and checking the mail and paying bills and—

Jake stalks past the bathrooms, his back to me.

I'm too surprised to say anything at first. He's walking with his gaze pointed straight ahead, his posture oddly stiff.

Normally, his movements are so loose, smooth, and unhurried. I don't know, something seems *off*.

He stops at a door at the end of the hall and reaches into his pocket, keys jangling in his hand. He inserts a key into the lock.

Nothing happens.

He jiggles it, then curses something under his breath.

"You okay over there?"

He spins around. "Ryan?"

I wave. "Hey."

"I-I didn't see you."

"I noticed."

He glances down at the keys in his hand. "I grabbed the wrong key ring. What are you doing over here?" His eyes roam over my position, lurking in the bathroom alcove.

"I came to visit Mom and then I had to—" I lift my hand to point at the bathroom behind me, then drop it. What's the point in lying? I've already unloaded on him enough times that he shouldn't be surprised by anything at this point. "I saw my ex and his pregnant fiancée, and I was hiding. If you want to know the truth of it."

His brows lift. "That sounds like a story."

I glance down the hall to the elevator where they disappeared moments ago. It slides open and I do a double take as lo and behold, Shane and Samantha step off. And they're heading this way.

Panic races through me.

"Why are they back? They're coming this way."

I spin around. I'll hide in the bathroom. But what if she came back down here to use this one? Maybe the one on the Ob-Gyn floor is full. Shit.

"Hey, come on. We can wait them out in here." Jake tugs me through a door between the two restrooms.

I catch a glimpse of open cabinets stacked with toilet paper and a mop before he shuts us inside and the room turns black, except for a thin bright line under the door.

It's a tight space. We aren't touching, but Jake's presence, the heat of him, is a substantial force behind me. My back faces him. I lean toward the door, tilting my ear toward any possible sound.

Ears straining, I catch only the murmur of distant voices.

"Did she go in the bathroom?" I whisper. "I didn't hear the door. You keep the hinges oiled too well."

"Are you going to tell me why we're hiding from your ex?" He shifts behind me, his shirt brushing my arm.

I let my forehead fall to the door with a soft thump. "I met Shane in college."

"In Ithaca?"

I nod. "He moved to Dull with me after Mia died. I was so grateful at the time." I rub my temple. I thought I was so lucky to have someone willing to give up everything and move across the country for me. Which was one of the reasons it took me so long to drop him. If it hadn't been for Ari, I might have married the asshole. I was so stupid. "We were together for four years."

"That's a long time."

"Yeah. We broke up because he didn't want kids."

He frowns. "But his fiancée is—"

"Yeah. She's pregnant." I wave a hand. "It doesn't matter. She can have him."

He's silent for a few long seconds. "So, you broke up because he couldn't handle raising a kid that wasn't his?"

"According to him, it wasn't that Ari wasn't *his*, it was that he didn't want kids at all. Except now he's having a baby and is all super stoked about it. It wasn't that he didn't want to be a dad . . ."

He didn't want me.

It hurts. Not because I want him back, but because . . . what's so bad about me?

"He's an ass. You are way too good for him. You dodged a bullet." His voice, low, calm, and assured, is as comforting as his words, like a soothing stroke down my spine.

"It was easier after we broke up, like I had one less child to take care of, one less person to worry about. I don't want to see him, or Samantha. They're difficult to talk to. It's exhausting. Maybe that sounds dumb."

"It's not dumb."

"I don't miss Shane, what I miss is . . . the idea of having a partner in life, you know? I thought he was someone I could grow old with. Someone to laugh with, cry with, share in the joys and the ups and the downs of parenting, and life in general. The exciting parts and the mundane day-to-day stuff."

Not to mention the fact that I would die to get laid. I haven't been with anyone since Shane.

Warm hands cover my shoulders, the heat of his chest brushing my back. "Hey. You'll have that someday."

Slowly, I turn around to face him.

His hands drop and then lift, sliding up my arms and cupping my face.

I wish I could read his expression. It's too dark to make out anything beyond the outline of his form.

"You're incredible, and someday, some lucky guy is going to love doing all the exciting and boring things with you."

Did he mean that to sound sexy? Because it did. Is he willing to participate in some exciting things with me? Because I am more than ready.

But I don't say that. I can't even think it.

I cover his fingers with mine. "Jake."

My phone dings and I jump away, banging my elbow into the door, the handle digging into my hip.

"Shit. I have to go. I have to pick up Ari."

"Okay. Maybe I'll see you later?"

"Yeah. Maybe."

I flee the storage closet like my ass is on fire.

"I'm hungry."

I finish wiping down the entertainment center and glance over at Ari. "I have a cereal bar in my purse."

She slumps back on the couch, crossing her arms over her chest with a huff. "I don't want that."

I grab the cleaning spray and move to the side table, squirting a couple of times before wiping it down. "I also have some nuts and dried fruit."

She grimaces. "You never have any good food."

I blow out a breath. When Ari is hungry, nothing will make her happy. I could put a giant cake and ice cream and a real live unicorn in front of her, and she would find something to complain about.

"I'm almost done with the dusting. I still need to vacuum. Then we can go home, and I'll make a pizza. How does that sound?" She loves pizza.

"Ugh." She falls over on the couch, covering her eyes with one arm flung over her face. "Fiiiiiine."

I do have that pizza in the back of the freezer still, don't I? A concern for a later time.

Fifteen minutes later, we're pulling into the driveway.

Ari is still cranky, complaining the whole five-minute drive home about how her shirt is itching her, her feet hurt, her eyes are dry, the house is too dark, and why can't we get a cat anyway?

I am so ready to get her into bed so I can breathe for a few minutes, and then we can start this whole dog-and-pony show all over again tomorrow.

Tomorrow will be better. It has to be.

Inside, I get Ari a glass of milk and then dig around in the freezer.

Please tell me it's in here somewhere. I move the box of chicken nuggets to one side.

"Momma, I spilled."

I wave a hand behind me. "Get the cleaning spray from under the sink and wipe it up."

Her footsteps shuffle against the linoleum, then stop.

I continue my search through a variety of frozen culinary delights like taquitos and peas and—is that bagel bites? Those are pizza-adjacent, right? I can sell these to her, maybe have a less volcanic reaction in my hungry child when I have to tell her the actual pizza is unavailable.

"Momma?"

The pizza is definitely not in here. Crap.

"Momma?"

"Yeah, Baby, it's the bottle with the blue liquid."

"It's wet all over."

"What?" I spin around.

Water is leaking out of the open cupboard and dripping onto the floor.

"Shit!"

I fall to a crouch in front of the sink and start yanking items out of the way. "Go get a towel," I order Aria.

She runs away and returns with a small washcloth, handing it over triumphantly.

I take a deep breath. "Maybe get a bigger one?" She'll come back with a dish towel next, no matter what I say. "You know, actually, will you go grab the red toolbox out of the garage?"

I know she knows exactly what and where that is.

"And a flashlight!" I call out as she disappears around the corner.

I peer into the dimness inside the cabinet, trying to locate the source of the leak and sigh.

I need to cut the water to the house. Maybe I can have Ari hold the towel to the leak, while I run and do that? Ugh.

These are the times I really wish I had an extra pair of adult hands.

Can this day get any suckier?

Chapter Ten

JAKE

"It's been over a week." Oliver's words lash across the phone line like a whip.

"It's only been a week and a half."

The menacing silence is almost more frightening than his words.

"I know, I know. I need a little more time. I'm almost done here."

Am I though?

I haven't found any big answers yet. And I don't want to leave. I'm not ready.

"Piper was deep in creation mode last week, but now she's coming out of it, and she's upset that you're gone."

I stifle a groan, covering my eyes with one hand.

Oliver will literally burn down the entire world if Piper so much as gets a paper cut.

I'm truly fucked now. Time is up.

"I am not okay with her being upset. You told me you left a note."

Wait, what? "I did leave a note."

"This note does not exist, according to Finley, who has even contacted Taylor."

Taylor is out of the country, on vacation in Greece with her boyfriend Atticus. "Just give me a little more time."

"No. Tell me where you are."

"I can't yet."

More ominous silence fills the line. "I'm going to find you." His voice is low and threatening.

I snort. "Okay, Liam Neeson."

A door slams and I lift my gaze to the house across the street. Ari bolts down the driveway. "You should really work on the Irish accent."

I frown. Why is she running?

She's heading this way, her blond hair and red cape streaming behind her. "Jake!"

I stand, checking up and down the street for cars.

"Piper is upset," Oliver says in my ear.

"Yeah, you mentioned that. She's my sister. I've upset her many times. She'll live. And I know you will find me, eventually, but I'm not telling you shit." Maybe that will buy me a few more days. "I gotta go, buh-bye now." I hang up and shove my phone in my pocket, approaching Ari in the middle of the street.

"Hey, is everything okay?"

"Come quick." She's already running back toward her house, calling out over her shoulder. "The water is everywhere, and I need to get the toolbox."

Water everywhere?

I jog to the side of the house, entering the backyard through the gate. The water key—a long metal instrument—rests against the side of the house. I grab it, sticking it down into the pipe to turn the valve off, and then sprint back to the front door, where Ari is lugging a toolbox half her size into the house.

I grab it from her and then follow into the kitchen where Ryan is on her hands and knees, sopping up water. Dish soap and bottles of cleaning liquid are scattered around her.

She looks up at me. "The water's off?"

"I turned it off."

Her expression is blank, her pallor tinged with gray.

"Momma, are you okay?" Ari frowns, a crease between her brows.

I crouch down by Ryan. "Hey. What do you need?"

Ryan leans back, the sopping wet towel in her hand flopping onto her knees. "I don't know. We were going to have pizza. I thought we had one in the freezer, but then I couldn't find it and then this happened." She gestures at the water covering the floor.

I clap my hands together. "Do you ladies want to roast some hot dogs out on the firepit?"

Ari's eyes widen. "We can do that?"

"If it's okay with your mom." I raise my eyebrows at Ryan.

She nods slowly.

I crouch down in front of Ari. "Why don't you run over to my house and grab the package of hot dogs from the fridge? There are buns on the counter too."

"Yes!" She lifts both arms in the air.

Ryan points at her. "Make sure you look both ways before crossing the street."

Ari scampers out the front door and I turn back to Ryan. She's staring under the sink like it might bite.

I crouch down next to her, putting a hand on her shoulder. "Hey. We can fix this."

Her eyes meet mine, and then her face crumples and she sags into me.

I wrap an arm around her, holding her against me even though the angle is a bit awkward, me crouched down on the balls of my feet with Ryan leaning into me from her knees.

Her shoulders tremble, but she doesn't make a sound. My heart breaks.

This is a woman who is shouldering the world by herself and refuses to crumble under pressure. She is so used to standing on her own. She needs someone to lean on. No one should be doing all she does alone.

"Why don't you go take a breather?"

Her hand grips my knee and she half laughs, half cries against my shoulder. "A breather? Are you kidding me? I don't even know what that means."

I shift back and straighten, taking her hand to help her stand.

"Go relax for a minute. Do whatever you need to do. The water is off. Nothing is urgent. The sink can wait until you both have food in your bellies. I'll feed Ari, and you can join us when you're ready."

She bites her lip, hesitant. "I can't ask you to do that."

"You're not asking. I'm doing it. I got this. You can let go for a minute. With any luck, maybe ten or twenty."

She searches my eyes, a clear battle waging across her face.

"It's so hard to be strong all the time. Sometimes you have to give a little, lean on someone. Getting help doesn't make you weak. It keeps you strong to fight another day."

She swallows.

"Ari will be back any second."

That stiffens her spine. She steps away from me and without another word heads down the hall. The door snicks shut right as Ari's feet tromp in the entryway.

I clap my hands together. "Let's go be cavemen." I thump on my chest. "Roast meat over fire."

She taps her chin with a finger. "Do cavemen wear capes?"

"It's literally a requirement. Do you have one for me?"

"My family owns a camp, and we do this all the time with the kids."

Ari's eyes are wide in the firelight, mustard dribbling down her chin while she shoves the hot dog in her mouth.

I turn the fork over the flames. We could only find one with a long enough handle to roast the dogs, so we're doing them one at a time.

"Can I go to your camp?"

"Maybe someday. It's a bit of a drive." Say, three thousand miles, give or take.

"Is it like my camp?"

I rub my chin. "I don't think so. You go to a day camp, right?"

"Yeah. They take us to the park and to the movies sometimes and we play games."

"At our camp, the kids stay overnight. Sometimes for a weekend, and sometimes for a week or longer. They sleep in cabins with bunk beds, eat in a mess hall, and do all kinds of things, like ice skating, paintball, hiking, fishing."

"What's a mess hall?" She takes a huge bite of her hot dog and ketchup plops on her shirt.

I hand her a napkin. "It's like a cafeteria."

She chews before speaking. "They have one of those at my school. I eat lunch there. They don't have hot dogs, but they have carrots."

I remove my hot dog from the fire and put it into a bun, then grab the mustard from the table and squirt a healthy dollop on it.

"You don't like ketchup?" Ari asks, her eyes tracking me as I take a bite.

I swallow my bite and shake my head. "My sister Taylor traumatized me."

Her eyes widen. "What did she do?"

"She dared me to chug a container of ketchup and it made me a little . . . sick. Haven't had much liking for the stuff since."

Ari laughs. "Where is your sister?"

"She's back home."

"At the camp?"

"She lives near there, yeah."

"Did you make her eat ketchup too?"

"Nah. I found other methods of torturing her."

She giggles, exposing the dimples in her cheeks.

I launch into stories about the pranks we played on each other, like setting Mindy's alarm to go off at three a.m. on the weekend, filling a Ziploc bag with red Jell-O and poking holes it in and stuffing it into Taylor's pillowcase, putting pebbles in each other's shoes—one time someone put maple syrup in mine.

"Our dad though, he was the ultimate prankster. His pranks went on for months, sometimes years." I chuckle.

"Where is your dad now?"

"He's . . ." What do you say to a kid when someone's dead? "He's in heaven."

Her eyes brighten. "My mommy is there too. Maybe they can play pranks on each other."

My throat grows hot and tight. I cough.

"I don't have a dad, but my friend Sophia has a dad. You kind of look like him, with your hair and your face." She motions to her chin. "Do you want to be a daddy?"

I rub the stubble along my jawline. "I uh, never really thought about it, but yeah. I would love to have kids, eventually."

It wasn't until the camp opened that I had much of an opportunity to interact with kids closely. But they're great. Funny, silly, brutally honest while also somehow managing to be complete liars, often frustrating, but at the end of the day ultimately pretty awesome.

"You need to find yourself a good woman."

A laugh bursts from my chest. "I guess you're right. You know where I can find one?"

"Did you save me any hot dogs?" Ryan steps through the back door. The strain that had marked her features a half hour ago is gone. Her hair is pulled back. She's changed into black leggings and a tank top, exposing the delicate curve of her collarbone and neck.

I swallow hard and avert my eyes, focusing on Ari as she flies up from the chair.

She races over to Ryan, wrapping her arms around

her legs. "We have a lot of hot dogs left. Can I cook yours?"

"I wouldn't have it any other way. Best chef I know." She leans over and kisses the top of her head.

Ari beams up at her. "Jake said we can go to his camp and stay the night and sleep in bunk beds and eat messy."

"Messy?" Ryan lifts a brow at me.

"In the mess hall," I clarify.

"Ah." She eyes me. "Nice cape."

Ari found a pink bed sheet for me to use, which I tied around my neck.

"You need a cape too, Momma. Cavemen roast meat and wear capes."

I bite my lip to keep my mouth in a serious line. "It's sort of the law."

Ryan chuckles. "Well, then let's go find me one before I break any laws."

They disappear inside.

My chest throbs. Not with the normal ache I've lived with over the past twelve years, but with something else entirely, something I don't want to probe too closely because I'm not staying and I'm not being completely honest with Ryan, or myself.

When they return, Ryan has a lavender sheet wrapped around her neck.

I hand Ari the long fork with the hot dog already speared on it so she can roast it for Ryan.

They start chatting about what movie to watch before bedtime. They normally watch *Bluey*, but Ari wants something less "babyish" now that she's all of six years old.

I half listen while inside, I'm at war with myself. I have to tell Ryan the truth. I have no idea how I'm going to tell Ryan the truth.

"What about *Adventure Time*?" Ryan asks.

Ari wrinkles her nose. "I want to watch a person show, not a cartoon."

I clear my throat. "Have you ladies ever witnessed the gloriousness that is *The 10th Kingdom*?"

Chapter Eleven

Ryan

By the time I emerge from Ari's bedroom, I half expect Jake to have bailed.

She took a quick bath, then we read *The Velveteen Rabbit*, and she had two "I have to pee still" episodes.

But he's still here, in the kitchen, putting all the cleaning supplies back under the sink.

"Did you fix it already?" Already. I've probably been in the back of the house with Ari for an hour.

In answer, he lifts the handle on the faucet and water gushes from the tap. He shuts it off. "It's fixed. There was an old, rusted fitting. It was simple enough to replace. There were extras in the garage."

"Thank you." I am always thanking him for something.

He wipes his hands on his jeans and leans back against the counter, crossing his arms over his chest. "Do you want to talk about it?"

"About what?"

"About your no good, terrible, awful, bad day?"

I snort. "Day? More like decade. You have six hours?"

One corner of his mouth quirks up. "I've got a couple, at least."

I sigh. "Do you want an apple or cranberry juice box?"

He claps his hands, rubbing them together. "How does one choose between such enticing options?"

I open the fridge. "We have more of the cranberry."

"Then it's settled."

"Wait. I have an idea so we can feel like real grownups." I spin around and open the cabinet behind me. On the top shelf are a few champagne glasses, dusty from disuse. I stretch up on my tiptoes to seize the nearest glass.

"Here. I've got it." He moves behind me, reaching over my head and pulling down two glasses.

He doesn't get close enough to so much as graze my back, and he's only behind me for a couple of seconds, but my nerve endings all come to attention like every cell in my body is suddenly alert and aware of his every movement.

He steps away, taking them over to the sink to rinse off the dust.

I squeeze the juice into the freshly rinsed glasses and

hand him one. We head back into the living room, which is cleaner than when I left it.

At some point, he must have straightened up. The crayons and coloring books that had littered the coffee table are all tucked away, resting on the corner of the table in a neat pile.

When I was grabbing the juice, the hot dogs were in a baggie sealed up in the fridge, which means he cleaned up the backyard at some point too.

It's such a little thing, compared to everything else he's done for me lately. Picking up a few things and putting them away—and yet somehow it hits me in the gut like a blow.

When I lived with Shane, I couldn't get him to clean up after himself, let alone pick up after me or Ari. He changed her diaper one time and acted like he saved the whole world, seeking praise like a giant manchild.

Jake is so different. He does it and doesn't point it out or ask for praise or expect anything in return.

Involuntarily, my eyes skip down the length of him as he crosses the living room, his broad shoulders, sinewy arms, tapered waist, jeans hugging his trim hips and outlining the curve of his—

"How was your visit with your mom today?" He settles onto the couch beside me. "We didn't get a chance to talk about it while we were hiding in the closet, but when I was fixing the light in the bathroom she seemed—"

"Off. I know. She has more and more bad days."

Then the words tumble out, more than I intend. It's like he's some kind of magician or wizard or something, able to draw thoughts and feelings from my being without my conscious assent.

In a rambling mess of thoughts, I explain how Mom became more alert and suddenly snapped out of her bad day with more clarity, but then she also hallucinated seeing Mia.

"It's a lot to deal with," he commiserates.

"It is. No one tells you about having an elderly parent with a debilitating disease. How it's like skating on ice. The sun is hot overhead, making the ice thin slowly beneath your feet. It's only a matter of time until it gets fragile, and you'll fall through . . . but even knowing what's coming, you can't leave. You're stuck there, waiting for the inevitable crack. Oh, and you don't actually know how to skate. After a while, you wish it would open up underneath and you could fall into the icy water and be done with it."

He reaches over, resting his fingers over mine, his thumb brushing the thin skin on the back of my hand.

I swallow hard and take a drink of my juice before continuing. "I miss her. I know she's still here, but it's not the same. I miss who she was before she got sick. She was invincible. After Dad died, she picked up the pieces of our lives. Even though Mia was in and out of hospitals constantly, she always made everything, even the hardest moments feel not so bad. She could handle anything. I can't even handle a leaky sink. Sometimes it's just so hard." I drag my gaze to his eyes, warm like dark honey.

He watches me, face unguarded, gaze direct. "Fuck."

I almost smile at that. "Yeah. Basically."

"So, you had an intense visit with Mom, then you almost ran into the prick of the year."

"Yep. To top it all off, Ari was pretty cranky this afternoon. I would have kept her at the day camp, but they closed early today and Priscilla had already scheduled some time off." I take a sip of juice from the champagne flute and set it on the table beside me.

"Do you ever take a break?"

"No."

He's silent for a moment, considering me. "Have you gone out with anyone since Shane?"

"Nothing more than a few crappy dates. I don't have time, but also, I don't want to bring anyone important into Ari's life unless I know it's serious."

"That makes sense."

His normally animated expression is carefully flat.

Insecurity grips me, heat rolling up my face.

And of course I open my mouth and ramble. "It's not that I don't want to date, but it's hard. I'm not exactly tripping over eligible bachelors in a town that is large enough that you can run into your ex every other day, but still date people who don't realize you have a kid and freak out about it."

His brows dip. "People freak out about you having a kid?"

"Oh, yeah. It's hard enough to be single. But with any kind of baggage? Forget about it."

He shakes his head. "People are assholes."

I really don't want to talk about my nonexistent love life. "What about you? Break a lot of hearts in Whitby?"

He chuckles. "Hardly. You definitely aren't alone with the lack of prospects. After my sister died, dating was the last thing on my mind."

"Of course. And then you took care of your dad."

He leans back, his hand lifting from mine. "Yeah. After that, I spent most of my free time at a bar. I met women there sometimes but," he blows out a breath, "it was never anything serious. The memories are hazy, and I wasn't ready to be anything to anyone. I haven't been on a real date at all since I've been sober. My therapist said I shouldn't even think about relationships until after a year of sobriety."

I rub a water spot on the stem of my glass. "How long have you been sober?"

"A year and eight months."

"Wow. Good for you."

The tips of his ears flush red. "Thanks."

I reach over and rest my fingers on his forearm. "Here I am, basically using you as my therapist since the minute you arrived, dumping all my problems and drama all over you."

I'm not used to having someone else I can rely on. I'm normally terrified to trust people, or let people in at all, but there's something about Jake that's different.

Maybe it's just his willingness to be vulnerable, to admit to his problems and how he's working on them and working on himself. Why is that so attractive?

Maybe because every other man I've dated has had the emotional intelligence of a gerbil.

"I don't mind being your sounding board. Everyone needs someone to talk to. Especially when you're raising a child alone. You're doing a great job. Ari is incredible."

I smile. "She is. The best thing I've ever done. I'm so worried about messing up somehow, doing something wrong. Mia isn't here and what if I screw it up?"

"You're not screwing up anything. You're doing the best you can."

"What if my best isn't enough? I'm not growing or changing. I'm not making my life better. I'm spending all my energy just holding on."

"Your best will be enough. I was raised by my sister, and it all worked out. Finley was only eight when our mom left, and she has been like my mom ever since. Through everything, every bad decision, every time I passed out at Veronica's and . . . she's my best friend. The one person I know I can always count on, no matter how much of a dumbass I am." He blinks, then frowns at the couch between us.

I look down, half expecting there to be a stain or something because of the look on his face, but it's the same old brown fabric it's always been. Not pretty or anything, but not necessarily "look of disgust" bad.

"Are you okay?" I ask.

"Yeah, I—I need to call her. I just realized I'm still being a terrible brother." He swipes his hand down his face.

"I'm sure that's not true."

"Oh, it's very true. I left Whitby sort of abruptly, without a proper goodbye." His head falls back onto the couch, and he considers me. "I'm not sorry I came here though."

My stomach flips. Is he saying what I think he's saying?

I grab my glass and take a sip of juice in an attempt to moisten my suddenly dry mouth. "Why did you leave Whitby? What made you pick Dull?"

He blinks and jerks his eyes from mine, picking up his own glass and taking a few deep pulls before setting it back down. "I needed to get away. I've spent my whole life in Whitby. I've never been anywhere else. My sisters, all four of them are in relationships and have been really busy with their own lives and I'm so happy for them. I want them to be happy but it's also a little . . ." His brow furrows as he waves a hand.

"Isolating?"

"Yeah. Exactly. I'm like a ninth wheel."

I laugh.

He shifts toward me, our knees brushing. "I needed to get away, you know? They are all incredible, supportive, and caring, but I've also put them through a wringer, and they feel like they need to take care of me and . . .

hover, I guess. I needed to take care of myself. To prove to them I could do it, but to myself too."

"Well from my perspective you're extremely capable of caring for yourself. Not to mention frequently having to rescue your extremely needy neighbor, who is also your landlady." I grimace. "Honestly, I feel like I'm taking advantage. You would tell me if you were uncomfortable, right?

"You're not taking advantage and I'm not uncomfortable at all." His eyes search mine and then snag on something to my left. "You have something." He leans forward, reaching for my hair and tugging on it.

My eyes trace over his features while he gets whatever it is out of my hair. Probably glitter, or lint, or fluff from one of Ari's many toys. He's only inches away. His eyes are focused on the task, his lips pursed.

His very full, soft-looking, kissable lips.

"Sorry," he murmurs. "I've almost got it."

The gentle pressure on my scalp continues.

He smells like cologne and soap with a hint of cranberry juice.

I swallow. Why is this turning me on? It's more than just the hair-pulling, it's him. Everything about him.

He holds up a small piece of white fuzz and grins. "Ta-da."

Before he can lean back, I tip forward and our lips meet.

Lust blasts through me, starting at my lips and racing

down to my toes. He tastes like cranberry juice and sunshine.

He jerks back. "Wait. I'm sorry."

I blink at him, slightly dazed. "What? Why?"

His expression is pained.

The lust quickly turns into embarrassment and shame. *Oh no.* I totally misread this. He's truly just being a nice guy, and I'm throwing myself at him.

If only the couch would open up and swallow me.

He frowns. "I should go."

I shut my eyes but the image of his wince after I kissed him is burned on my retinas. I'm such an idiot. He told me he doesn't date. It's been more than a year since he's been sober, but maybe he's not ready yet. And here I am, making assumptions and being . . . horny. "I'm really sorry. I thought—I totally misread that and now I'm really embarrassed."

"It's not—please don't be embarrassed. I wanted that kiss. More than I should want it."

"What do you mean?"

His eyes search mine. "I . . . we haven't even been out on a proper date. Can I take you out to dinner?"

Wait. "What?"

"Dinner. You know, that thing where two adults eat good food somewhere other than their home with no children present and something slightly more upscale than hot dogs?"

He doesn't want to kiss me, because he wants to *date* me first? Is he for real?

122

So that distressed look wasn't because he's disgusted with me? I didn't know men like this existed.

"Um, Ari has a sleepover at her friend's this weekend. Maybe then?"

He grins, and my stomach dips. "It's a date."

Chapter Twelve

JAKE

"Hey, Donuts. What are you doing?"

I jump at the unexpected voice behind me and spin around.

My heart, already frantically pounding as I attempt to inconspicuously break into Elaine's office while she's at lunch, triples in speed.

"Sorry." Bernie scrunches her nose at me. "I didn't mean to startle you."

"It's fine."

She glances at Elaine's door, then down at my hand on the knob, brows rising in question. "Are you busy?"

"I just needed to grab an HR form. What's up?"

Bernie reminds me of my sisters. She's an amalgam Taylor's sassiness and Mindy's ball-busting and Finley's kindness. We hit it off right away, though not in the same way I hit it off with Ryan . . . My life might be less complicated right now if I were more attracted to Bernie, instead of the woman I've come across the country to investigate and lie to.

"You're taking Ryan out tonight?" she asks.

My mind takes a second to catch up to the question. "Yeah. Why?"

She puts one hand on her hip. "Is this like, a date?"

If Ryan hasn't told her, I'm not going to be the one to do so. "Why are you asking?"

Her brows lift and then she straightens, stretching her five-foot-nothing height as tall as it will go. "Ryan has been my best friend since before puberty. If you string her along or hurt her, I know twenty-five ways to kill a man and I have a four-body trunk."

I frown. "Do you need a four-body trunk to murder just little ol' me?"

She shoves me in the shoulder. "I mean it, Donuts."

I lift my hands. "Listen, Bernie. I like Ryan. And Ari. I would never do anything to hurt either of them."

Guilt pushes at me. Am I already hurting them? Or about to, once I come clean?

I've had dinner with her and Ari every night since the sink incident earlier this week.

Last night, I treated them both to pizza after running into them here at the hospital when they came to visit Ryan's mom. We ate, played games, and watched more of *The 10th Kingdom*. We're only a couple episodes in, and

Ari is as obsessed as my sisters and I were when we were kids.

Every night, I fully intend to come clean about the real reason I'm here in Dull. Lay everything all out there. But every night I can't. The words stick in the back of my throat. So, it's still there, sitting between us like a giant immovable rock, growing in size, and I am the only one aware of it.

I haven't been staying to hang out with Ryan after Ari goes to bed. It's not just because of my avoidance to telling the truth. Ryan is clearly exhausted from running herself ragged day in and day out. It would be cruel to impose myself on the only time she has to herself to relax. I can't kiss her again without telling her everything. And I can't be alone around her without wanting to kiss her.

The need is a drumbeat in my veins.

I'm making excuses to avoid dealing with consequences.

Because consequences suck. But I can't keep it a secret much longer. There will be no perfect time. Logically, I know all this, and yet when I'm hanging out with my girls it's . . . that's just it. They feel like "my girls" and I have no right to it. And as soon as I tell her the truth, it will be over.

"I'm glad you're taking her out. She deserves a nice dinner." Bernie's voice snaps me back to the conversation. "It's been a rough week. You know her mom is deteriorating pretty quickly."

"I know."

A nurse calls her name down the hall, and she has to run to check on a computer issue, waving at me over her shoulder as she strides away.

I blow out a breath and then open Elaine's door.

I grab an HR form from the wall randomly, just in case someone walks in and asks questions, then I carefully open the drawer and grab the keyring.

Elaine only goes out for lunch once a week. The last time I attempted to get into the locked scanning room with all the files, I ran into Ryan. This time, I have to get it done. I may not have another week before my family descends and forces me back home. Honestly, I'm surprised someone hasn't shown up on my doorstep already. I slip the keys in my pocket and then check my watch. I have about twenty minutes until Elaine gets back.

My hands are shaking. I barely register the ding of the elevator when I reach the bottom floor.

Glancing around, I move as fast as my shaking hands allow, sticking in one key after another until finally I reach one that works.

Eureka!

Elation bursts through me but there's no time to celebrate.

I shut and lock the door behind me, then flick on the lights. On the table at the back of the room sit two dark computer monitors with a scanner in between them. Lining the walls to the left are beige file cabinets, each about five feet tall. I stride over, singing the alphabet song in my head as I scan the labels. There. *GRE-GRO.*

Sliding it open, I flip through the files until I find it.

Green, Mia

My stomach flips, heart accelerating.

Guilt whispers through my gut. I shouldn't be doing this. But I have to do this. I might not even find anything useful, but I have to check for . . . something that connects Mia to Dad. Anything.

I open the file, skimming through the details, flipping through the pages. Basic biographical information. A record of the congenital heart defect, tricuspid atresia. Fontan procedure given at six to divert the flow of blood around the right ventricle. More follow-ups and hospital visits, and records transferred from Ithaca . . .

I glance at my watch. Ten minutes. I need more time.

The connection has to be in New York. I flip to the Ithaca medical reports, and then my eyes snag on the date of a major surgery—a familiar date, over twelve years ago.

The day Aria died.

I reexamine the details, and then realization flows through me, letters and numbers blurring on the page.

Mia had a heart transplant.

I didn't know. No one mentioned a transplant, only her heart condition.

The same day Aria died, Mia had a heart transplant.

We were close in age. Aria and I are only a year older than Mia. Aria was fifteen, Mia was fourteen.

Rushing white noise fills my ears.

Ryan wrote letters to my dad about Mia. Did Dad— did he? Was Aria's heart donated? To *Mia*? He never said anything. Why didn't he say anything? Why wouldn't he tell me?

It's my fault. We never talked about Aria. Every time he tried to bring her up, I changed the subject.

Why didn't he tell Finley? Why didn't he tell *anyone*? Wait. Maybe he did tell someone. Why wouldn't they tell me?

My mind is tripping down rabbit holes, creating questions I cannot answer.

It's too much to take in. I can't think straight. I close the file and slip it back into the cabinet, my fingers shaking.

Breathe.

I suck down a few long deep breaths, taking time I don't have to calm my body before I exit the room.

The walk back to Elaine's office is a blur. Somehow, I get the keys back into her desk without being stopped or questioned along the way. Then I slip into a stall in the nearest men's room and attempt to pull the pieces together.

What the hell do I do now?

I stare at the back of the stall door. Minutes pass. I keep breathing until my body settles and my mind clears enough to think somewhat straight.

Sliding my phone from my pocket, I pull up Dwayne's number and shoot him a text, letting him know what I found out. Mia had a heart transplant the day Aria died. Maybe he can find more out for me, now that we have this little tidbit.

This is definitely the reason Dad was exchanging letters with the family and explains why Ryan always told stories about Mia in her correspondence, but I only had the one side of the story—I never had letters from Dad to Ryan.

Does she still have the letters?

I need to tell her everything.

She's going to hate me.

Maybe I'll pull her aside before dinner. During dinner? With her mouth full so she can't yell. No, after dinner.

I can't think straight.

I still have to get through the rest of this workday.

Eventually, I leave the bathroom and put one foot in front of the other and make it back to the break room to clock in when my lunch period ends. Then I go through the motions of the day, doing my best to pretend like my whole world hasn't been rocked on its foundation.

Bits and pieces of Mia's medical file float through my consciousness. She was at the top of the transplant list because she was going to die.

If Aria hadn't died, Mia might have. If Mia had died, then little Ari wouldn't be here.

That's why they named her Aria. Mia knew the name of the teenage girl whose death saved her life.

Ari. Aria. Shit. If Aria hadn't been in the accident . . . *fuck.*

"The address labels were printed, and there was no return address because the transplant center would ship the letters back and forth between them."

I pace back and forth in the front room of the rental, my phone pressed to my ear. Dwayne texted me back a couple hours ago, letting me know he had more info and I've been crawling out of my skin to get off work and get home to have this exact conversation.

"Why didn't they exchange the letters directly?"

"Because Ryan was a minor at the time. With adults, they will allow direct communication after going through a consent process. Donor recipients send thank-you notes all the time, but because Ryan was under eighteen and it was ongoing, they needed a go-between to ensure privacy and that's why they used first names only and didn't disclose addresses on either side."

I rub my jawline, exhausted from . . . everything. I stop pacing and look out the front window.

Ryan's little Honda isn't there. She must be taking Ari to her friend's house for the sleepover. She only lives a few blocks away. She should be back soon for our date.

"Thank you. For everything."

"If you think of any other questions I can answer, you know how to reach me."

We hang up right as Ryan pulls in front of her house.

I glance at the clock. I have about an hour to get ready.

Guilt hammers me from all sides.

For lying to Ryan. For all the times I wished Aria were still here. Because if Aria were still here, Ari might not be. Life is so bizarre. So many choices piling together, leading to inevitable outcomes. Like the butterfly effect.

What-if scenarios crowd my brain. What if Aria hadn't died? Would Ari still exist? Would I be here now? Would I have met Ryan at all? Not likely. These thoughts are pointless. I *am* here now.

After Aria died, the scant minutes here and there when I wasn't numb with shock, my thoughts constantly hummed around what I could have done differently. If only I had convinced Aria to not go to the party. If only we had waited for Taylor to drive us home. If only, if only, if only. But I can't go back and change anything. Maybe it's true, if I had done something differently that night, the outcome would have been different. But I didn't. And it wasn't. And here we are.

Grief is love with nowhere to go . . . but now it has somewhere to go. Maybe. Do I deserve it?

Fifty minutes later, I'm crossing the street, mind racing. This is it. This is an opportunity to tell her the truth. And . . . completely ruin her evening.

But it needs to be done. There will be no good time to do this. I have to tell her tonight. Ari won't be there, and we'll be alone so she can yell and scream or kick my ass if she wants to.

I knock on the door and check for the eleventh time that I've buttoned my shirt up correctly.

The door swings open.

My mouth goes dry.

I've seen Ryan dressed casually, jeans and T-shirt, in her work clothes, stuff that can get dirty, and relaxing clothes like sweats and leggings.

My eyes dip down and back up. She's wearing dark jeans, a silky black top that slips off one shoulder. Her hair is down and slightly curled, her lips are shiny, and she's in heels.

Fuck.

She's a stunner when we're sitting on the couch with Ari and she's fresh-faced with her hair pulled back and a tomato sauce stain on her shirt. But this . . .

"You're fucking gorgeous."

Her smile lights up the whole night. It reaches into my chest and grabs my heart and squeezes.

And by the end of the night, she's going to hate me.

Chapter Thirteen

Ryan

I bite my lip and glance down at the heels I slipped on at the last minute to add some glitz to the rest of the outfit. They're just black strappy heels with a smidge of sparkle, but I haven't worn them in years. Haven't had a reason.

"Is it too much?" I put on mascara for crying out loud. I had to dig into my bathroom drawer and find it, and I was lucky it wasn't completely dried out.

Now I'm reconsidering everything. As I was getting dressed, it wasn't enough, and now I'm thinking it's too much, although we're well matched since he's also wearing dark jeans and a dark gray button-up shirt that's nice without being overly done.

Jake hasn't made a peep. His hair is damp and

brushed back from his face. He swallows. "Not too much. Amazing." His eyes are warm with appreciation.

Everything inside me melts.

"Are you ready?"

"As I'll ever be."

Jake grins, the brightness driving out any lingering doubts I had about this whole thing.

I lock the door and follow him to his truck.

Flutters spread from my stomach to my limbs, my whole body warming with an awareness I haven't experienced in years. Maybe a decade. I don't even remember the early days with Shane anymore, the whole relationship tainted by the end of it.

The feelings for Jake snuck up on me. He's been eating with us every night this week, bringing over pizza, being wonderful with Ari and solicitous and kind and all things amazing, but he hasn't made any moves. Not since the other night when he asked me to dinner, but I don't think it's because he doesn't want to.

He opens the passenger door and helps me climb in, his warm fingers surrounding mine for a couple of seconds, and just that fleeting moment sends heat racing up my arm, nerve endings flaming.

I shift in the bench seat. "Where are we going?"

"InDullgent Bistro."

"Oh, nice. I've heard it's good."

"You haven't been?" He flicks the blinker on, checking the blind spot before switching lanes.

"I don't generally eat in places without built-in play areas."

He flashes a quick smile in my direction. "When was the last time you went on a date?"

I dip my head, rubbing a worn spot on the strap of my purse. "I did go on a lunch date a couple weeks ago. It was . . . not great."

"What happened?"

I tap a finger on my chin. "Let's see, he chewed with his mouth open, spit while he talked, made sexist comments about the waitress, and showed up that same night at my place—to return my wallet, which I had accidentally left at the restaurant—and tried to invite himself inside. Until he spotted Ari and ran for the hills."

"Ooh. Yeah, I saw him."

My eyes widen. "You saw him?"

"That was my first night here. I heard the car door slam and looked out the window." He winces. "Maybe I should have looked away. I didn't hear anything, but you looked kinda uncomfortable, so I kept an eye out."

"Ah. Well." I shrug. "Thanks."

"The guy sounds like a total dickhead."

I chuckle. "That's what Bernie said, except using the word dick at least a dozen more times."

He turns into the parking lot. "Well, I promise to chew with my mouth closed, make a valiant attempt not to drool in front of you, and I'll only make sexist comments when I think you aren't listening."

I laugh. "Perfect."

He parks his truck, turning it off and then pointing at me. "Don't move."

I lift my hands. "Wouldn't dream of it."

He jogs around to my door and takes my hand again to help me down.

This time he doesn't let go, his fingers weaving through mine as we walk toward the restaurant. My stomach dips, my skin tingling from the contact.

InDullgent Bistro doesn't look like much from the outside, situated at the end of a strip mall, next to a tax preparer office and pet groomer, but it is the nicest and newest restaurant in town.

Inside though, it's easy to forget the shoddy exterior. Large, plush booths line the periphery of the dining area. The wooden tables are polished to a subtle sheen and set with linen napkins and shiny silverware.

We follow the host around the well-worn dance floor and to our table. Laughter and quiet conversations fill the space. Jake's fingers are a light pressure on the small of my back as we weave through the building.

Once we're seated and we've put in our drink orders —tea for me and soda for him—I have no idea what to say. My mind blanks. My heart is beating too loud in my ears. How do people do this with people they actually like? What if I open my mouth and say something stupid? More stupid than the past times I've opened my mouth and wordgitated all over him. A fake flickering candle sits on the table between us. I stare at it and fidget with the menu.

Jake reaches across the table, his hand covering mine. "Did I ever tell you about how I got into cross-stitch?"

A surprised laugh gurgles out. "Cross-stitch?"

"It's kind of a funny story."

He launches into it, telling me how Archer—his sister's boyfriend—was hell-bent on finding activities to distract him from wanting to drink and forced him into anything and everything he could think of, from bowling to fishing . . . to cross-stitch. Which was supposed to be CrossFit, but something got lost in translation.

While we're talking, the waiter comes over to read us the specials and takes our orders.

When he leaves, Jake leans back in the seat, considering me. "We've talked so much about our crappy pasts, I haven't heard enough about all the other things."

"What other things?" My life has been entwined with tragedy. It's like wading through a thick swamp, trying to dig for the good that's been buried under the weight of the sad.

"Like, what's your favorite color?" he asks.

I consider the question for a second. "Black."

He blinks. "Black? Seriously? That's not even a color."

"Uh, it's technically all of the colors."

He shakes his head. "It's depressing. I said non-crappy things."

My mouth pops open. "Are you calling my favorite color crappy?"

"Again, not a color."

I scowl at him. "It is too a color, and it goes with everything. What's your favorite color?"

His eyes search mine. "I used to think it was green, but now I think it might be blue."

I bite back a smile. I have blue eyes.

It's so cheesy. If anyone else threw out that line, I would roll my eyes or make a sarcastic comment, but when Jake says it . . . it's real. I can't explain it, it's just different.

He drums his fingers on the table, getting back to business. "Next question. What's the best gift you've ever received?"

I give him the first memory that pops to mind. "Last year on my birthday, Ari brought me breakfast in bed. Since her culinary skills were that of a five-year-old, I ended up with a glass of milk, a granola bar, and a banana. And she spilled half the milk all over the counter." I chuckle. "She also gave me a report card."

"And how did you rate?"

"Straight As, of course."

He grins. "Of course."

I straighten in my seat. "Okay, what about you?"

He rubs his chin. "Hmm. Best gift." He snaps his fingers. "It was from Archer. He bought me a blanket."

My brows lift. "A blanket? That's the best gift you've ever received?"

"It was an oversized blanket with his face printed on it."

I burst out laughing.

We go back and forth for a few minutes about various likes and dislikes, favorites, least favorites, and then guilty pleasures.

I wrinkle my nose. "I don't know. It's kind of embarrassing."

He snorts. "I'm not ashamed. I love K-dramas."

My mouth pops open in surprise.

He shrugs. "They're too good to miss. Romance, drama, excitement, what's not to love? Now your turn."

I chuckle. "Liking K-dramas is not that bad."

He shifts in the seat, leaning toward me. "Well, now I'm really curious. Is yours very bad? Are you a nose picker?"

A startled laugh escapes me. "Oh, gross, no! All right, lest you think I enjoy picking my nose and eating it . . . my guilty pleasure is that I really like to daydream."

The corner of his mouth twitches. "That's it? Daydreaming?"

I lean forward. "It's more than that. I like to vividly daydream entire scenarios and conversations and different realities, like I'm rich and donating a bunch of money to people in need, or I'm a world-class athlete at the Olympics, or a famous singer impressing a crowd." My face burns and I lift my hand to my head. "It's weird, right?"

A grin spreads across his face and some of my discomfort ebbs. "No. I think it's normal, actually. I fantasize about beating Oliver all the time at . . . anything, really."

I laugh.

"Do you ever fantasize about applying to a nursing program again?"

I take a sip of my tea and try to ignore the pang of regret and frustration lancing through my gut. There's no point in fretting over things I can't control. "I wish. It could never be more than a fantasy. I can't leave Dull. I can't move Mom, and there are no nursing schools nearby, even if I had the time."

"But what if all barriers were removed? Assume you have no other responsibilities."

"In that fantasy world? Yes, of course. In a heartbeat. It was my dream. I wanted to be a transplant nurse."

His gaze sharpens on mine. "Because of Mia?"

I fiddle with my napkin. "They do regular nursing care, but they also coordinate everything for the transplant, working with recipients and their families through the whole process. The nurse we had was incredible. It made a truly daunting experience so much better, you know, to just have someone that could keep us informed and be there from start to finish."

He leans back in the booth seat. "Seems like it would be a really fulfilling job."

"Absolutely." And a way to honor my sister's memory and everything we went through together. Having family in and out of hospitals all the time has been a living nightmare. But the nurses and other hospital staff who have worked with Mia and Mom have made the most awful situations bearable.

His head tilts. "You all moved to Ithaca because of Mia's condition?"

I nod. "Yeah. There's only the one hospital here, and they wouldn't have been able to do a transplant if an organ became available. We would have had to get to Portland." I blow out a breath. "It was too far. Organs have a specific timeframe where they need to be transplanted, and hearts are only viable for four to six hours. Mia needed more than Dull could provide, even on a regular basis. So, Mom found a job in Ithaca, and we moved."

Our food arrives, ribs for Jake, salmon for me. We eat in silence for a minute, but it's not strained. My earlier nerves have vanished, but awareness still throbs between us.

"Then after Mia had the transplant, she moved back to Dull?"

I spear a bite of mashed potatoes. "Yes. A couple years later. I stayed behind for college."

He wipes his mouth with a napkin. "Did you plan on moving back to Dull after graduation?"

"No. I never wanted to come back. At least, not permanently. Dull has never really felt like home to me. But when Mia got pregnant and started having complications, I had to return."

"Why didn't you go back to Ithaca after Ari was born?"

"Mom got sick. She didn't want to leave Dull. Mia

and Dad are buried here and . . ." I trail off and shrug. What other choice was there?

Music fills the space, a slow, folksy song. The band is only two people, a man and a woman on guitar and piano, harmonizing together with limited instruments, so the volume isn't overwhelming. Couples trickle onto the dance floor, swaying slowly.

He watches me, his lips turning down. "I have to admit, I'm a little irritated on your behalf that your dreams were put on hold—not because of Mia or your mom, they couldn't control the circumstances any more than you could. It's complete bullshit you couldn't follow your dreams, you know? Sometimes you can do everything right and still lose out and it's just . . ." He shakes his head. "It's so unfair."

I stare at him, struck speechless by his understanding, by his ability to verbalize thoughts and emotions I've had for years, but have been unable to express. It is unfair. Life can be so unfair.

He is definitely getting laid tonight.

Chapter Fourteen

JAKE

Her cheeks pinken. She sets her fork down, her eyes dipping down to her lap before lifting to mine. "You're right. It is unfair. But saying that, or even allowing myself to admit it feels like it's somehow dishonoring what my family has gone through. How could I have been selfish about nursing school when my baby sister was sick and dying? How can I blame my mom for being sick and incapable of caring for herself?"

I reach over. I have to touch her. I put my hand over hers. "You can't. I know."

A surge of understanding and recognition passes between us. It's like a silent conversation. Time stands still. I can't tear my gaze away. It's more intimate than a kiss. We've been kindred spirits all along.

The moment is so intense, I can't help but laugh.

Then we both laugh.

She swallows and shakes her head, her eyes shifting down to her handbag. "Excuse me for a minute. I need to call Ari to say good night before it gets too late."

"Of course."

She winds through tables, and as soon as she rounds the corner toward the restrooms and disappears from view, I rub my hands down my face.

Did that totally freak her out as much as it freaked me out?

I'm telling her everything. Maybe when we're on our way back home. No, not while I'm driving. I don't want her to feel trapped, and she might want to get as far away from me as possible.

As soon as I park the truck in front of her house, I'll tell her. Just put it out there. Then she can yell and scream and hit me in private before running away and possibly evicting me.

I have to find a way to make it up to her.

I like her. So much. Too much.

We have this . . . connection. I can't even explain it. Telling her the truth is going to ruin it, but I can't keep it from her. Not anymore.

The waitress comes back with the check, and I pay it before Ryan returns. I hope she is okay. Hopefully everything is okay with Ari.

I glance around the room until my eyes snag on

Ryan. She's standing beside a table halfway between our table and the entrance, talking to someone.

Her smile is strained, even from this distance.

I scan the table's occupants. It's the couple from the hospital, her ex-boyfriend and fiancé.

I slip out of the booth seat and head in her direction.

"Hey, there, I missed you." I slide my arm around her waist and dip my head, speaking low in her ear. "Did you need an assist?"

Her hand covers mine on her waist. "Uh, this is Jake. Jake, this is Shane and Sam."

"Samantha." Her nostrils flare.

Cute.

"Right. Hi. I see you are both enjoying a date night like we are." I grin down at Ryan.

She's gazing up at me, mouth partially open, a bird caught in a trap.

"We're celebrating my pregnancy." Samantha beams at Shane.

Shane is staring at me, frowning.

"Congratulations. Kids are incredible. They change your life, you know? I love spending time with Ari. The kid's hilarious."

Samantha's head bobs emphatically in agreement.

Then Shane opens his mouth. "Yeah, she is great. I was there when she was born, you know. I changed her diapers and held her at night when she cried. I'm her Uncle Shane."

I narrow my gaze on him. The filthy liar. "Weird. She

never talks about you. And she had a birthday last weekend. You weren't there. So even if you were there when she was born, you're not doing a great job of sticking around for her, Uncle Shane." I can't keep the sarcasm from spilling into my tone.

His eyes widen, his mouth puckering like he just sucked on a lemon. "I can't always be there for a child who isn't mine."

I pause and stare at him, counting to ten.

Ryan tenses even further beside me. In a minute she's going to start vibrating she's so rigid.

I wait until his words have truly sunk in for everyone at the table. Samantha shifts, still smiling, but the edges are forced and strained.

I moderate my tone, keeping it even and unemotional. "Anyone can make a child, but few have the courage to raise one. It is my privilege to be a part of her life, and I feel sorry for anyone who can't see that."

I dip my head to speak low in Ryan's ear, already putting this interaction and this douchebag out of my mind. At no moment did he ever deserve Ryan. "Do you want to dance?" Damn, she smells good, the bright floral notes of her perfume tickling my nose.

Her hand covers mine, and she grips it firmly. "Yes. Please."

Without another word to the couple at the table, I whisk her onto the dance floor.

Her arms go around my neck, fingers brushing my nape.

I draw her close. It's a slow country song that I've never heard, but it might be my new favorite. We move together among the rest of the swaying couples.

"Are you okay?" I murmur.

"Yes. Thank you for the rescue."

"I hope I wasn't overstepping. I know you wanted to avoid them at the hospital, and I was trying to help you make a getaway, but if I—"

"What you said, about Ari, about being a parent, did you mean it?"

I blink down at her. "Of course."

She swallows. "Thank you. You know, you're kind of amazing."

I preen, pretending to toss my hair over my shoulder. "I had to go through a lot of being an immature asshole to become the stunning man you see before you."

She laughs.

"I'm not perfect." I swallow. "I've made plenty of mistakes, in the past and more recently." Things I still need to inform her of. My stomach twists with nerves. This is going to suck.

"Everyone makes mistakes. It's part of the human condition. We are all learning and growing and figuring this whole life thing out."

I really hope she's this understanding and forgiving later.

She leans in, resting her head on my shoulder.

I want to freeze this moment in time, take it out when this is all over, so I can reexperience Ryan in my arms, the curve of her waist against the sensitive pads of my fingers, the scent of her skin, the way she relaxes against me, warm and trusting.

I'm a fool. An idiot. I deserve all the guilt thundering through me.

The song ends and her head lifts.

My hands flex around her waist. "Are you ready to go home?"

"Yes."

The drive back is quiet.

As we draw nearer to her house, my anxiety intensifies, reaching a crescendo by the time I park. My palms are clammy. I grip the steering wheel tightly, the weight of anticipation heavy in my gut.

Moment of truth.

I kill the engine and shift to face her. Her gaze is directed down, unclipping her seat belt.

"Ryan, I have to tell you, I—"

She scoots across the bench seat, reaches up and grabs my face with both hands, and presses her mouth to mine.

I freeze. I can't move. I can't let her do this.

Her mouth moves against mine. Her lips are soft, warm, probing.

Holy hell.

Heat blasts through me and then I'm kissing her back. More than mere kissing. Devouring.

Her hands move down my face to my shoulders.

I cup the side of her face, tilting her jaw for better access. She tastes like honey and lemon and heaven. Her tongue slides against mine and every blood cell in my body rushes south.

Brain has left the chat.

I need more, more of her flesh under my mouth. My lips graze down her neck, moving down to her collarbone and biting gently. She groans and the sound shoots straight to my cock. The most erotic noise ever made.

She gasps. "I want to feel more of you."

Yes.

She tugs my shirt from my pants and then her fingers brush against the sensitive skin of my stomach. Now I'm the one gasping.

"Not enough," she murmurs.

Not nearly enough.

She leans back and whips her shirt over her head.

I stare, open-mouthed. She's all soft skin and subtle curves and she's wearing a black lacy bra that's mostly see-through and *fuck*.

Her hair is wild around her face, her eyes drowsy, lips swollen.

Beautiful.

Reaching forward with one hand, I trace the tips of my fingers over her lips. Her tongue flicks out against the pad of my thumb, and I shudder.

Swallowing hard, I trail my touch down, over her collarbone, then cup her breast in my hands.

Heaven.

Her breathing is ragged. "Jake. We need to go inside."

The words penetrate through the haze of lust clouding my mind.

I can't go inside. I shouldn't have gotten sucked into this moment. I should have told her the truth immediately.

Her hand runs down my chest, cupping the bulge between my legs and I suck air in through my teeth.

No.

I rest a hand over hers. "Ryan. Before we go inside, I need to tell you something."

Her eyes fly up to mine. She blinks, wariness slowly overtaking lust in her expression. "Oh. Okay."

She releases me, moving back a few inches. I want to eliminate even that scant distance, reach for her, hold her hand or something, but if she touches me again, I might not be able to get through this.

"The real reason I came to Dull was to find you."

Her head jerks back. "What?"

I scrub a hand through my hair. "I wasn't completely honest when you asked why I was here in Dull. I did want to leave Whitby for all the reasons I told you, that wasn't a lie, but I left out the thing that brought me here in the first place."

She shakes her head, bewildered. "What are you talking about?"

"My sister, my twin, the one we talked about . . . the one who died." I swallow.

She nods slowly, watching me with wary eyes.

"Her name." I stop and swallow. I've only said her

name once since she passed, and it was an accident. This is the first time I've said it, out loud, willingly. "Aria. Her name was Aria."

She doesn't say anything. Her face is blank, emotionless, like a statue.

My heart is pounding.

Is she even breathing?

I keep talking. "I found your letters. The ones you sent to my dad about Mia after her transplant. He never told us about the heart donation. I didn't know. I only had the letters and there wasn't much in them to understand the relationship, and I didn't know why you were writing to him, and I-I had to know. I came here to find out why and . . . now I know."

She lifts a hand. "Wait. Hold on. I don't understand. Your sister, your twin who died. Your twin was Aria? *The* Aria? The one who—?"

"Yes. I just made the connection, today."

The silence beats down on my head while she searches my eyes in the dim light and the puzzle pieces click together in her mind.

"You lied to me."

I wince. I can't deny it.

"Why?"

I swallow, mouth dry. "At first I was surprised when you weren't a dude, and then I wasn't sure if I should just ask or if I should wait to see if we were related—"

"You thought we were related?" Her voice is shrill.

I wince.

"How did you—if you just made the connection about the heart transplant today, how long did you think we were related and how did you figure out we weren't? Assuming you kissed me after you determined we were," she waves a hand, "genetically variant."

I rub my chin. "Well, that's a funny story, actually." I frown. I do not want to tell her about digging through her trash.

Damn. I really messed this up.

I stare out the windshield into the dark street, struggling to find the right words to explain why I'm a complete moron.

But then she speaks in hushed tones.

"Is that why you're doing all this?" Her voice breaks on the last word. Her eyes are wide, mouth turned down.

"Doing all what?"

"Pretending to like me."

Something in my chest cracks. "No. No. Not at all it's not—"

Her back straightens. "You lied to me."

I can't deny it. But . . . "I also told you truths I've never shared with anyone else."

"How am I supposed to believe that?"

I have no response.

Her eyes are wet and full of hurt and it's my fault.

Without another word, she picks her shirt up from the seat between us and slips out of the car, shutting the door behind her without force, like it's a normal end to the night and she's going inside and my whole world hasn't just been smashed to pieces because of my own bad choices.

Fuck.

I sit in the car for a few minutes, maybe longer, just staring out the window. My body aches with the guilt. This hurts. I wish I could escape into a bottle of something strong and stinging, but I immediately push the thought aside. When you have a problem and you drink, now you have two problems. I know this. I've learned this. I'm better than this, even if right now, it's hard to believe.

Eventually, I get out of the truck and walk across the street toward my rental.

There's an unfamiliar car parked out front. A dark midsize sedan.

And movement on my front porch.

"Are you hooking up with your neighbor?" a familiar voice calls out.

Shock halts me in my tracks. "Finley?"

Chapter Fifteen

JAKE

"You didn't have to come all the way out here." I sit on the couch.

Finley hands me a mug of tea and plops down beside me.

It's only been twenty minutes since I found her on my porch and she's already smacked me upside the head, burst into tears, hugged me for five minutes straight, inspected the contents of my kitchen, and made us two mugs of chamomile tea.

"Well, you weren't returning my calls so of course I did. You just freaking took off. I've had so much work to do at the camp, I would have been here sooner but I had to make sure everything was covered before I just bailed because not all of us have that luxury." She smacks me in the shoulder.

"Would you stop hitting me?"

She hits me again. "When you stop deserving it. That one was from Oliver. He said to tell you he wasted three whole days trying to find you and Carson wasted one day, not because he's smarter than Oliver, but because he's just as ridiculous as you, which is to be taken as the insult it is."

I rest my head back against the couch. "I deserve much worse."

She lifts her mug to her lips, blowing on it before taking a sip. "Now tell me everything. Start with the reason you didn't leave me a note."

"I left a note."

She gives me the side eye. "The Post-it that fell on the floor and got kicked under the fridge does not count as a note. We just found it a few days ago."

I set my cup of tea on the coffee table. "I didn't know that would happen. I didn't want you to try and convince me to stay or talk me out of it or come with me. I had to do this myself."

"You can make your own decisions, Jake, but for god's sake tell someone where you are. You can be a man who stands on his own and still inform the people who care about you. To their face."

I wince.

"Now." She takes a breath in and out. "Who was the woman you were making out with?"

"You saw that?"

She nods. "I watched your truck pull up and park across the street. I approached, thinking you would see me, but then realized what was happening and quickly retreated."

"That's Ryan."

She stares at me blankly. "Ryan?"

"The person who was writing Dad those letters."

She blinks rapidly. "Wait. What?"

"Oliver didn't tell you?"

She groans. "I'm going to kill that man. But you first. Go."

I tell her everything, going back to over a year ago when I hired the PI and figured out where the letters were coming from. I explain how the PI found the obituary for Mia, and how Ryan was listed as her surviving sibling. How I spent months checking and waiting for a job to open up locally and striking pay dirt when it finally happened at the hospital where Mia worked, and the rental was also available for an extended time.

I detail all my theories, and how I was able to negate some of the more obvious ones, like the DNA test. I describe little Ari, Mia's daughter. Then I explain what I discovered about the heart transplant and how I just tonight dropped the bomb on Ryan about why I was really there and what brought me to Dull.

"Did Dad ever mention anything about the heart donation?"

She shakes her head slowly back and forth, confusion marring her brow. "I had no idea. Why didn't he tell us?"

"I was going to ask you the same thing."

She stares blankly at the coffee table, and I wait, letting her process everything.

After a minute, she speaks. "I can't believe Aria's heart was donated to someone, and we didn't know. Dad received letters from her, and he never said anything. Why wouldn't he say something?"

"It's my fault. I would never let him talk about . . . anything."

She rubs my arm. "It's not your fault. He could have told me or Mindy, and we could have told you when you were ready."

"He was also dying of cancer and had other things to think about."

"True." Her eyes soften and she leans into me. "It's still not fair to you, Jacob. You were with him all the time, taking care of him. He should have told you, even if it was hard."

Heat fills my eyes.

I don't know what it is about Finley. It's like things don't hit me until she's a part of it.

Like when I was six and I fell off the jungle gym at school and got the wind knocked out of me. It was terrifying, but I was so proud of getting up on my own and not crying. Then Finley came over from the high school on her lunch break. As soon as I saw her walking across the grass, I started sobbing like an infant.

I swallow. "Finley, I'm so sorry."

She whacks me on the arm again. "Good. Maybe you'll think twice about taking off like that again."

I scrub a hand through my hair. "It's not just for that. I am sorry I left like I did. I'm also sorry about all the years of drinking and behaving like a jackass and taking advantage of your kindness. I'm sorry for all of it." I'm sorry about what happened twelve years ago, for the part I played in the loss of our sister, but I'm not going there. "For everything I've done, or not done, all of it, really."

She throws her arms around my neck. "Oh, Jake. I know. I know if you could change the past, you would. But we can't. We're here now though, and even though I'm still very pissed at you, I'm also really proud of you. You don't need to apologize, because there is nothing to forgive. We've all been affected by the past. We've all made mistakes. We can't change those things, but we can move forward together and try to be better. That's all it's really about, right?"

Right.

I have to try and be better for Ryan. I have to find a way to make it up to her. Not because I want forgiveness, although I do, but it isn't about me.

She pulls back, patting my shoulder. "The mystery is solved. Now you can come home."

"Yeah. I can."

There's no reason for me to stay.

Her eyes narrow at me. "You want to stay, don't you?"

Having siblings who can read your mind is both a blessing and a curse.

She speaks into my silence, answering an unspoken question. "It's because of Ryan."

I nod. "And Ari."

She shifts on the couch, angling her legs toward me. "You know, whatever you decide, we'll support you. And if you leave, I'll call daily and visit at least twice a month."

I chuckle.

"Maybe once a month."

The thought of never seeing Ryan or Ari again is like a knife to the chest. What if she doesn't forgive me? I wouldn't blame her if she never wanted anything to do with me ever again.

"Ryan hates me."

"Like you've ever let a little thing like pure, undiluted hate stop you before. Remember when Piper got her first cell phone and you kept leaving notes on people's cars that said *sorry for hitting your car* along with her number, except no one had actually hit the car and there was zero damage, so she was getting a million calls a day? And you were only ten."

I laugh. "She was so pissed."

"Yeah, but she forgave you."

"After I groveled, agreed to admit all culpability on her voicemail for anyone who called, and did her chores for a month."

"You are stubborn and loving and a good person. Good people can make bad decisions. You'll win her over."

"I hope you're right."

We talk for a couple of hours. Finley catches me up on what's been happening at home with the camp, Archer, wedding plans, Taylor's trip to Greece with Atticus, Mindy's tour schedule, all of it.

I convince Finley to sleep in the bed for the night, and I take the couch.

It's late. It's been an emotional day. I should be exhausted, but I can't sleep.

My mind spins over everything. Finley is leaving early tomorrow. She needs to get back to camp. I'm going to be following up behind her, after putting in notice at the hospital. My lease here is up next week anyway. I never intended to stay.

Then why does the thought of leaving tear me up inside? I need to find a way to make it up to Ryan and Ari.

Somehow.

"This is disappointing news. I'm really sorry that you're leaving us so quickly."

"I am too. I apologize for any inconvenience."

Elaine waves a hand. "It happens. I understand family obligations."

I rub the back of my neck. Here I am, lying again. But I cannot tell Elaine the real reason I'm leaving, especially since it affects Ryan. Another lie to add to the list. Or half lie. I do have to go home because of family, but I invented an emergency. I never intended to stay, so I knew this was coming, but the guilt is still there—just more to add to the pile.

I scoot forward in the guest chair, resting my forearms on her desk. "There's one thing I wanted to ask you about."

Her head tilts to one side. "Of course."

"Mrs. Green, in room 410? I was wondering if I could pay some money toward her balance owed."

Elaine's brows lift so high they disappear under her bangs. "You want to pay for her cost of care?"

I rub the back of my neck. "Or a portion of it. I don't know what's owed, but I have some money set aside that I would like to put on her account balance. The only thing is, I don't want Ryan to know it was me. If you could tell her there was an accounting glitch or something, that would be great."

She clucks and eyes me, then she nods. "You heard what happened then? Word gets around fast. I just called Ryan about an hour ago."

My skin prickles. *What?* "What happened?"

Her brows dip. "You didn't hear?"

I shake my head. "Hear what?"

"Mrs. Green passed this morning."

I rock back in the chair. Damn. After the bomb I laid on her last night, her mom died.

Fuck.

Chapter Sixteen

RYAN

The ringing phone jerks me from a dead sleep at five o'clock in the morning.

I've only been asleep for a few hours, since I spent most of the night making sense of Jake's confession and looking for the letters I had received from his dad, Ted. That was his name. I never knew his last name. They're in a box somewhere in one of our closets.

The letters petered out years ago, and I only remember bits and pieces. I don't recall him mentioning his other kids. He was funny though. And he was so happy that a piece of his daughter, Aria, was out in the world, living and loving and growing. He was like a kindly uncle or something. Connecting those memories with what Jake has told me is like this weird shift in reality and the cognitive dissonance is still ringing in my ears. He's dead now. Not only did I spend last night grieving who I thought Jake was, I also had to grieve that realization too.

Groggy and confused, I fumble for my cell phone on the nightstand. Is it Ari? What if something is wrong?

"Hello?" The word is a croak.

"Ryan?"

I blink at the shadowed bedroom around me, clearing my vision and trying to comprehend the voice on the other end of the phone. "Elaine?"

"I'm so sorry honey. She's gone."

I rub my eyes.

The words don't register. Gone? Who's gone?

Then clarity strikes. It slices through me, a hot blade through my already thin skin.

"What?"

"She passed about a half hour ago, in her sleep. I'm sorry for calling so early, but I knew you would want to know right away."

My hands are numb. Emotion floods through me, sorrow, denial, pain, and some relief followed up with a smack of guilt.

My skin is ice and fire and ice again.

We hang up. I think I say goodbye, I don't know. Everything is blank. The shadowy room is lightening to gray as the sun rises and peeks through the cracks in the curtains.

I need to go to the hospital and figure out what the

next steps are. I need to pick up Ari. I need to explain to her that her grandma is gone, and she's not coming back.

All of life's little dramas become insignificant in the starkness of losing someone you love forever.

I can barely fathom the endlessness of it. People die and they just aren't there again, ever. It's an unfillable hole.

I need to get up. I need to take care of . . . everything.

It's like a pile of boulders falling on top of me, each one heavier than the last. It's all so daunting. I thought I knew it was coming. It was inevitable. We planned for it. But dragging myself out of bed is suddenly an impossible task.

I have to get through this day, go to the hospital, sort out whatever needs sorted, then pick up Ari, and let her know what happened. I have to be strong for her.

Thoughts of my girl give me the strength to push myself out of bed. I go through the motions. Shower. Get dressed. Make coffee.

Everything takes forever. It's like I'm moving through wet concrete.

I take one sip of coffee and chuck it in the sink. My stomach is a mess.

Leaning against the kitchen counter, I check the time. It's after seven. Not too early for parents of young children. I text Michelle.

She replies quickly. The girls are still sleeping.

I breathe in and out then type a message letting her know that I have to stop by the hospital before I pick Ari up and I'll be there on time. We already agreed I would come get her by lunch. I had hoped this morning would be spent in bed with . . . Jake.

My eyes shut. I can't think of him right now.

I can't think of anything. I stand there for I don't even know how long with my eyes closed.

A brisk knock at the door makes me jump.

I steel my spine. What if it's him? Part of me hopes for it, part of me dreads it.

The knocks come again, rapid fire. "Ryan?"

My shoulders droop. Bernie. Of course.

I open the door and she throws her arms around me. "I heard. I'm so sorry."

I wish I could collapse against her. I wish I could rage, scream, cry at the unfairness of it all, but I can't. Not yet. There is work to be done, so I let her hug me, and I pat her shoulder and I try not to take the comfort for too long. I can't, not without completely losing it.

"I came to drive you to the hospital."

"I can—"

Her hand flips up, palm facing me. "Shut all the way up. You are not driving right now. You are not doing this alone."

My eyes fill and I blink back the tears. "Thank you."

When we're both seated in her bright yellow Mini Cooper and halfway to the hospital she says, "Jake put in his notice early this morning. Did you know?"

"I figured."

"This may not be the best time to ask, but what the hell happened?"

I give her a recap of the evening, all of it delivered in monotone, like it's someone else speaking right now and I'm only listening, removed from the events. I describe the amazing conversation at dinner—most of it, anyway. I don't reveal his personal details since his story isn't mine to tell. Then running into Shane, every perfect thing he did and said . . . all leading to the aftermath. Everything Jake told me about why he's really here, how his sister was Mia's heart donor, and he had no idea except for the letters I had sent to his dad.

By the time I've filled her in on everything, we've been sitting in the parking lot of the hospital for ten minutes.

"That's . . . I can't believe it."

"He literally got a job at the hospital, rented the house across the street from me, drove across the damn country to, what, make me fall for him and then act like every other asshole I've ever known but a thousand times worse?"

Bernie purses her lips. "Hmm."

"What does that mean? You can't seriously be on his side."

"I'm not on his side." She reaches over, putting a hand on my arm. "I'm always on your side. Always."

I lift a hand. "But? Go ahead, I know you're thinking it."

"But . . . he has been through a lot, just like you. And

I can see why he would wonder about the letters to his dad, and it's not like he could have asked his dad, and it would have been really awkward to just show up and be like 'hey, remember how you exchanged letters with a middle-aged man in high school? Also, why?' "

"He should have told me when we kissed the first time."

"You're right. He should have. He screwed up, big time. But maybe you should hear him out."

"I know what he'll say."

He tried to tell me. He stopped us the first night we kissed because he wanted to tell me the truth. He stopped us last night when I invited him in.

When I put myself in his shoes, I can almost understand it. I understand why he wouldn't immediately ask about the letters, and how not asking right away would put him in the position of making it harder and harder the longer it dragged on.

"But he came to my house. We had hours-long conversations about everything I've gone through. He had no problems being vulnerable about his life, about the death of his sister, about so many other things. He helped me with my sink. He hung out with Ari and he, and he—"

"He made you think he was everything all your ex-boyfriends were not."

"Yeah."

"He did come clean though, eventually."

It's that eventually that stings.

"Do you think you can forgive him?"

"I don't know. Am I weak for wanting to?"

"No. Never."

"I'm not ready to think about him. I need to deal with," I gesture to the hospital, "whatever needs to be done."

She puts her hand over mine. "Hey. You aren't alone in this, okay? We'll deal with it together."

I swallow back the tidal wave of emotions, shoving them down into a box, locking it up, and swallowing the key. There will be time for that later.

The days after Mom's death are a blur.

All of her end-of-life planning was detailed out and paid for years ago, so that part is almost too easy.

Now, a week later, the day of the funeral has arrived faster than I thought possible. It's a small, quick affair, with less than twenty people, local friends and acquaintances, plus a half dozen staff from the hospital. It's held at the local cemetery. Mom is laid to rest next to Dad and Mia. It's a beautiful day. Sunny, the sky dotted with fluffy clouds. The air is thick with sunshine and the smell of sweet, fresh-cut flowers, but my mind is only partially present.

I barely remember the past week, with a few stand-out moments.

Like when Elaine told me half of Mom's cost of care

had been miraculously eliminated because of some funding grant.

"It's a thing people do. You know, a charity that pays for people's medical care."

"But . . . wouldn't someone have told me? What's the name of it?"

She brushed off my questions. "It's a secret thing, you know."

I don't know, but I don't have the energy to argue with her. Plus, it's a huge relief.

The next memorable event is when I relay the news of Grandma's passing to Ari. I waited until we got home from her friends, told her we needed to talk, sat with her on the couch, and just laid it out there. With kids, it's best to stick to the facts and be clear.

"Grandma died. As you know, she's been sick for a long time. We won't be able to talk to her or see her anymore. But we have so many good memories, and we can always talk about her, whenever you want. She loved you very much."

She frowned. "I'll never see her, ever again?"

"No." And isn't that the rub? "She's gone, sweetie."

She sighed. "She's with Mommy now. I bet Mommy is happy she gets to see her again."

My heart twisted. "I bet you're right."

The rattle of the crank as Mom's coffin is lowered into the earth jerks me back to the present.

After the brief service is over, most of the attendees follow us home, bringing casseroles and plants and flowers, all the things that are supposed to somehow help you deal with profound loss, along with platitudes like *I'm so sorry for your loss* and *If there is any way we can help.* How can anything help? No one can stop death itself.

But then I think *fuck* and remember Jake, and the darkness ebbs, a little.

He's leaving soon. His rental contract is up in two days.

He left a letter on my porch yesterday along with a brochure for Camp Aria.

He didn't tell me the camp was named after his sister. In fact, now that I think of it, he never said her name, not until the end. He really went through a lot of trouble to avoid saying her name—but I get it. I've gone through periods, especially right after her death, when I struggled to say Mia's name.

I've read the note so many times, I've nearly memorized the contents.

I'm sorry. For my mistakes, and for the loss of your mom. I know an apology doesn't make anything better, and it doesn't take back what I did, but I wanted to give it to you anyway. I won't bother you. But if you want to talk or punch me in the face, you know where to find me.

If you need to escape Dull for a weekend, or a week, there's a bungalow in Whitby with your name on it. Just say the word.

. . .

Ari has asked about Jake three times. Each time, I deflect and change the subject or tell her I don't know. I did tell her that he won't be living here much longer. She stopped asking. The thought of him leaving, of moving back across the country, is both a relief and a regret. It's the regret that kills me. I have to talk to him before he leaves, if only for closure.

As for his offer, getting away from Dull and going literally anywhere would be absolute heaven. But I couldn't possibly go to Jake's family home with him. It would be so strange, wouldn't it? Visiting where Aria and Ted lived? Being around Jake and the rest of his siblings? Also I haven't forgiven him yet.

Yet.

Does that mean I want to?

I still like him. I hate that I still like him.

He may have had reasons for his deception, he may have attempted to be noble, but he took my DNA without my knowledge, for crying out loud.

How can I possibly move past that? Every choice I make affects Ari too.

By the time everyone leaves, and Ari and I are alone, I'm dead on my feet. I put on *Bluey* and sit next to her on the couch, not bothering to clean up the plates and cups scattered around the house.

It can all wait.

After fifteen minutes of staring at the TV with no real awareness of anything, except for Ari's warmth burrowed into my side, she turns to me.

"Momma?"

"Yes, baby?"

"Is real mommy in heaven because of me?"

I freeze, muscles tensing, breath stuttering to a halt in my chest. "Why would you think that, baby?"

"That lady with the weird hat that was here earlier said if Mommy hadn't had a baby, she wouldn't have died. Aren't I her only baby?"

Tears burn the backs of my eyes.

It's too soon for this conversation. She's six years old. I thought I would have more time.

"First of all, your mommy wanted you more than anything. She did not die from having a baby. She died because she was born with a bad heart. That wasn't anyone's fault. Having you was her happiest moment. She faced the end with nothing but peace knowing that you would live on when she couldn't. You are made of everything that was best about her. You did not take her from this world. You are how she remains in it."

She frowns at me, a little divot between her brows, and says nothing.

I swallow. Does this even make sense to a six-year-old? "Do you understand what I'm saying?"

She nods slowly. "I think so." She's quiet for a few seconds. "You might have to tell me again later."

"Okay, baby." I rub her shoulder and kiss the top of her head. *Maybe when you're twenty-five.*

She snuggles deeper into my side. "When is Jake coming over to finish watching our show?"

My chest aches. He was streaming it from his phone. I could probably find it myself, but Ari would never allow us to watch it without him. "I don't know, sweetie."

"Can you ask him?"

"He might be busy. He's leaving soon."

"Please?"

I should talk to him before he leaves. I'll regret it if I don't. It's not fair to Ari to keep him at arm's length when she might never see him again. She deserves to be able to say goodbye. Eventually, I will have to explain to her about how Jake's twin is her namesake. She knows a little about how her name is very special, how it came from a girl, an angel, who saved her mom's life.

"I can go check, but you need to stay here, okay?"

It's a testament to how tired she is that she doesn't argue and instead lies down on the couch without a word of protest.

"I'll be right back."

I walk across the street, my mind turning over the past, the present, the unknown future. My stomach spins with nerves. Maybe I shouldn't be doing this. Maybe I should turn around, go back inside, tell Ari he's not home or he's sleeping or something.

But I don't.

I reach his door and after only a few seconds of hesitation, I knock.

Ten heartbeats later, the door swings open.

"Hey."

Damn he looks good. He's wearing jeans slung low on his narrow hips and the same dark blue T-shirt he wore when I came over to fix the stove, and he's never looked more enticing.

Even though his eyes are tired, his face tight with strain, something in me relaxes at the sight of him. It's like the chaos of the past week stills, and a puzzle piece slots into place. At the same time, the concrete walls I've been fortifying around my heart shift, a crack stretching over the surface.

"Hi," I manage to get out.

"Do you want to come in?"

"I can't. I left Ari watching TV and I . . ." I don't have to explain.

He crosses the threshold and a whiff of his scent—just simple soap and aftershave—reaches into my midsection and tugs.

I step back and cross my arms over my chest.

He doesn't say anything. He waits, devouring me with those deep brown eyes, his gaze a caress against my skin.

To my horror, my eyes burn and my face heats, the crack in the dam around my emotions fracturing.

A sob bursts out of me. My hand claps over my mouth.

Then his arms are around me, solid and warm, and all the barricades I've erected and strengthened over the past week dissolve in the face of his comfort.

Chapter Seventeen

JAKE

She's falling apart in my arms, and I'm helpless to do anything but hold her and wait. I wish I could take all her pain into myself, but I can't.

I rub her back, press my lips against her hair and murmur nonsense while she shudders and shakes and sobs in my arms. I know these tears are about more than my revelation last week, but I still wish I had the power to remove the sting of my lies, along with everything else.

I bet she hasn't cried since it happened. She wouldn't want Ari to witness this.

My body aches for her.

We stand on the porch for a while, until her tears subside and her shoulders stop shaking and she pulls away, wiping at her face. "This is so embarrassing."

I clench my hands at my side so I don't give in to the urge to reach for her, or brush her hair away from her face, or pull her back into my arms. I don't have the right.

Her eyes widen and she turns her gaze across the street. "Oh no. I have to get back."

"Do you have any time to talk before I leave?"

She swallows. "Ari wanted to watch more of *The 10th Kingdom*. Can you come over now? Maybe we can talk when she goes to bed? Unless you have to pack or something, I understand if—"

Relief swells through me, leaving me almost light-headed. "Now is great. Perfect. I just need to grab my shoes."

She nods. "Okay. I'll leave the front door unlocked." With a weak half smile, she jogs down the porch steps.

In a daze, I grab my shoes and keys and follow.

Pushing open her door, I follow the sound of murmured voices into the living room.

I stop in the doorway. "Hey, superhero."

"Jake!" Ari leaps from the couch and runs to me. I lift her up and her little arms immediately wrap around my neck and squeeze.

A tidal wave of raw tenderness washes over me from head to toe. I missed her these past few days, Ari and Ryan.

She pulls away slightly. "My grandma's dead."

"I know."

She hugs me again, holding my neck tight.

How can I just go and never see them again? I'm not ready to say goodbye. I set her down on her feet.

"Are we going to watch more of our show?" She tugs on my arm, leading me over to the couch and directing me on where to sit so she can crawl between Ryan and me.

"Absolutely."

I put it on and then try to relax.

Ari leans into my side, tucking her feet up against Ryan's thigh.

I'm intrinsically aware of Ryan's presence, only a couple feet away. What is she thinking? What will she say when we get a chance to talk? It can't be too terrible if she's allowing me to be here.

On the screen, the characters are in a place called "Kissing Town." Wolf is wooing Virginia, trying to get her to fall in love with him. It's incredibly cheesy and silly, but I've always enjoyed this part the best. Of course, Wolf has been lying and withholding information from Virginia since they met. He's been working for the evil queen since episode one.

The parallels to my current situation are not lost on me.

After the episode ends, it's time for Ari to wash her face and brush her teeth before bed.

I wait in the living room, wiping sweating palms on my jeans and going over and over in my mind what to say to make it better.

By the time Ari's door snicks shut, I still have nothing.

Ryan's footsteps sound in the hall, moving into the kitchen. The fridge opens and shuts. When she appears in the doorway to the living room, she's holding two juice pouches.

"She is exhausted after everything today. I think she might stay in bed this time." She hands me one of the drinks.

A smile tugs at my mouth. "I see we're moving up in the world."

She sits on the other side of the couch, tucking her legs up underneath her. "From boxes to pouches. We're so posh."

We lapse into silence. The fridge hums. A car door slams outside in the distance. The quiet stretches and wraps its arms around me, squeezing tighter and tighter until I have to break it.

I take a few pulls on my juice pouch, unsure what to say, where to start. I guess with the truth, no matter how shameful it is. "I went through your trash."

She blinks. "What?"

I grimace and rub the back of my neck. "For the DNA. When you came over to fix the stove I . . . it was me that unplugged it. I wanted to meet you."

The groove between her brows disappears. "The water. You kept offering a water bottle."

"Yeah."

"I thought that was weird."

"I couldn't think of another way to get something. So, that night after the stove thing, I came over here and . . ." I tilt my head toward the wall.

"You went dumpster diving?"

"Yes. I'm not proud of it. It was invasive and I was stupid and I should have just told you everything right away instead of being a coward."

I can't look at her. I stare down at my hands. I can't handle the derision that could be in her eyes. How can she ever forgive me, or trust me again?

Then Ryan speaks, her voice low and steady. "I understand why you didn't tell me right away. I just wish you would have told me sooner."

"I know. You're absolutely right. I screwed up. I wish I could go back and change it, but I can't. But I promise, full disclosure going forward . . . if there is a forward."

Please let there be a forward.

She doesn't say anything. She frowns at her juice pouch for so long, I wonder if someone pushed the pause button on my life.

"Bernie said you were asking about me."

"Um, what?"

She waves a hand. "Before. When you first came to town. She said you were asking people at the hospital about me, and Mia, and Mom. I thought," she shakes her head, "I thought it was because you were into me, not because you were . . . investigating why I had written letters to your dad. I feel like an idiot now."

Regret twists through me, sharp as any blade. "I'm so sorry. I'm the idiot, not you. You weren't wrong."

"What do you mean?"

"I did like you. I still like you. I don't want this to be the end. The thought of never seeing or talking to you or Ari again is tearing me up inside."

She sets her juice pouch to the side, her knee bouncing up and down for a few seconds before she speaks again. "Did you want to see the other letters?"

That question knocks me back on the couch. "The other letters? The . . . the ones Dad sent you? You have them?"

She stands up and leaves the room.

I lean forward, resting my elbows on my knees and my face in my hands.

She's not kicking me out. That's something positive to hold on to. Maybe I can convince her to at least stay in touch.

Dad's letters. I can't even imagine—

She returns, handing me a dusty shoebox. There's no lid.

I set it in my lap, staring down at the folded letter at the top, the familiar blocky handwriting.

The same handwriting that signed my school papers, left notes on the fridge when a chore needed to get done, and scrawled our names on the labels of our presents on Christmas morning. The loss strikes me upside the head all over again. Grief is like that. You think you're all fine and safe and then something inside you becomes aware of the absence of their presence, like a physical pang, a phantom limb pain.

"Mostly he would write about Aria. There are lot of funny stories about her in there. He didn't mention you, or the rest of your siblings. I don't know why. Maybe since Aria was the one who connected us." She shrugs one shoulder.

I rip my eyes from the letters and look over at her. "Thank you." My voice is gruff and scratchy.

Her eyes soften. "You don't have to read them here and now. Take it with you."

"I can't—"

She waves me off. "You can send them back to me whenever you're ready."

"Are you sure?"

"Of course."

My fingers tighten around the box. "Thank you."

I don't think I'm entirely forgiven. She hasn't said as much. But this box in my hands is way better than a slap in the face or a jab in the eye. Not that I expected Ryan to suddenly turn into one of the Three Stooges, but still. The kind gesture is surprising.

If only she'll let me reciprocate.

"Have you thought about it? Coming to Whitby for a visit?" Or forever? I won't mention that yet. Starting small seems like the wisest course of action. Baby steps.

She shifts on the couch, crossing her legs. "I don't know."

Hope lifts in my heart. "That wasn't a no."

"I have work."

"Could someone else cover you for a few days?"

"Maybe."

"When was the last time you took time off?"

She blows out a breath. "Hardly ever. I only took a few mornings off even this week to get mom's affairs in order."

"You need time to rest. Relax. Everything would be taken care of. We have plenty of cabins, all meals would be covered, plus there is so much to do. Ari would love it. We can go fishing, hiking, axe throwing. Literally anything any kid could want to do, it's there." I bite my lip to stop the words from going on and on and talking her out of it.

"You have no idea how tempting that is. Ari with an axe might be a bad idea, however, but I don't know. I'd have to see if someone could cover me at work."

"It wouldn't hurt to ask."

"I guess not. But I can't really afford to fly across the country, even if meals and lodging are free."

I scratch my chin. "Well, if you can go in a couple days, you can just ride with me."

She's shaking her head before I even finish my sentence. "Driving would be way too long—"

"I'm not driving. Remember Oliver the billionaire?"

"Piper's boyfriend."

"Right. So, at his insistence, his private jet is picking me up at the Portland airport in a couple days. It can definitely fit two more."

Her brows fly up. "Private jet? What about your truck?"

I wave a hand. "He has someone meeting me at the airport to bring it back to Whitby."

She stares at me. "Are you serious?"

"I know it's weird. You get used to the whole snap-his-fingers-and-things-just-miraculously-happen thing. Actually, no, you don't really get used to it. Either way, it's all taken care of."

"Just like that?"

"Just like that."

Her mouth opens, then closes. Then opens again.

"Ari would freak out over the plane. Can you imagine her reaction to it? To everything?"

She chuckles. "Low blow, using Ari, but Jake, I can't possibly accept such a gift. I would have to pay for something."

"Fine. You can reimburse us for the food."

She sighs. "I don't know."

The hope deflates like a pricked balloon. Maybe it's a bad idea anyway. I'm already in too deep. I like her too much. We live on opposite coasts. She can't trust me and that is not a good foundation for . . . anything. I don't even know that she likes me that way, anymore.

It's probably a recipe for disaster.

She rubs her lips together. "I have to think about it."

Thinking about it isn't a no. I'll take what I can get. "I understand."

I'll wait. As long as it takes. I'll grovel and apologize

and crawl over broken glass, anything I can do to make it up to her. I'm not giving up.

Chapter Eighteen

Ryan

It takes five days, three dinners with Jake, endless begging from Ari, and two conversations with Bernie before I finally make a decision.

Since Jake's rental agreement expired and we had another tenant moving in, he decamped to a motel in the center of town.

He wasn't staying to pressure me, but because he was training his replacement at the hospital. He planned on heading back to Whitby by the weekend, whether I had made my decision or not.

"You can change your mind at any time," he insisted. "A month from now, two months from now, or tomorrow."

The three times he came over for dinner throughout

the week, we didn't talk about his Whitby offer at all. Instead, we finished watching *The 10th Kingdom*, then discussed our favorite fairy-tale stories, which segued into favorite superheroes and superhero powers and what powers were the best and why.

"I want to fly. Like Superman and Doctor Strange and Captain Marvel," Ari told us, her tone very serious for a six-year-old who also had chocolate frosting smeared across her face, since Jake brought over cupcakes for dessert.

"I want to be able to control the elements like Storm and Magneto," Jake said.

They both looked over at me. "I think teleportation. I could blink and be anywhere in the world."

He left shortly after dinner each night, with a smile and a wave and no pressure.

I wanted him to pressure.

If we don't go, I will regret it.

Which is why we're now at the Portland International Airport, staring up at a private jet.

"I know you said Oliver was a billionaire and we would be going on his private jet, and I understood all that in theory, but I don't think I truly grasped it until this moment." Not to mention all the preceding moments. Like when we drove to a secluded area of the airport, parked in a side lot, and were escorted in a black sedan straight onto the tarmac.

Who needs to be felt up by TSA? Not us, apparently.

I glance down at Ari.

She gapes at the steps leading up to the sleek white plane. She hasn't talked much this morning. Maybe she's tired, since I woke her up at six to get here by nine, and we were up late last night packing because she wanted to bring her entire closet for a three-day trip and I had to convince her to narrow it down a bit.

Jake has been a lifesaver, distracting Ari during the drive when she was cranky, bringing extra snacks and drinks, factoring in time for bathroom breaks and buying more snacks along the way when Ari said she needed something sugary to help her wake up.

"You ready, superhero?"

"We're going up there?" She points at the plane.

"Yep. Do you want to meet the pilot?"

She nods slowly.

"Most planes are bigger than this, but they also fly a lot more people," Jake explains as we climb up the steps. "Like two hundred people. We get this whole plane to ourselves."

Ari's first flight and it's a private jet. Who would have thought?

It will be a quick trip. We're spending three nights and two days in New York, spending one day in Whitby and at least part of one in Ithaca, so Ari can see where both her moms lived for a time.

The pilot greets us at the door, standing near the open cockpit. She has sleek blond hair pulled back into a bob and she's wearing a black suit. "Welcome aboard," she says, shaking our hands as we enter the plane.

"Thank you," Ari says politely, shaking her hand and then moving farther inside. She looks around, her eyes wide, and I'm sure I have an even more awestruck expression on my face.

The sun is shining through the windows, intensifying the brightness of the gold and white interior. A long sofa lines one side across from a row of sleek cream leather seats and shiny wood desks. In the back, steps lead up to a closed door. Another room?

"Where do I sit?" Ari asks.

"Wherever you want." Jake gestures broadly. "You can pick first."

She purses her lips and then walks over and sets her backpack in the middle of the couch, her eyes as wide as saucers. "Will you sit with me?"

"Absolutely." Jake grins at me over her head, clearly enjoying her awestruck, wide-eyed gaze.

I'm melting inside. I don't want to. I want to hold on to the wariness so that I don't fall for Jake more than I already have.

I'm still so attracted to him, I ache with it.

At the last minute, before we left the house, I stuffed a box of condoms in my luggage.

It might be the stupidest thing I've ever considered. It can only be temporary. We live on opposite sides of the country. I might never see him again. And yes, he lied, by omission, but in spite of that, I trust him. At least, enough to bring me to orgasm.

Because I'm an idiot? Maybe. What am I thinking?

I'm thinking I haven't been laid in years, I haven't been attracted to a man in years, and this might be my only chance before I die alone.

The door in the back of the plane slides open.

"Jakey!" A woman rushes out, running into Jake and hugging him hard.

He opens his arms and holds her tight. "Hey, Piper, I didn't know you would be here."

Piper Fox. The artist. She and Jake have the same dark hair and the same dark honey eyes.

She pulls back and then smacks him in the arm. "If you ever leave again like that I will . . . I don't know, something bad."

"I'm terrified," Jake says, his voice dry.

"You should be." A man appears in the doorway.

He's shorter than Jake, sleek and trim, in a three-piece, navy-blue suit, but he's got this palpable energy waving off him like he owns not only the plane but the whole planet. This must be Oliver.

Jake groans.

Oliver stalks toward him. "Did you really think I wouldn't be here?"

"A man can hope."

Oliver glares at him, crossing his arms over his chest. "We need to talk."

Ari tugs on my hand. "Momma, I have to go potty."

All three gazes whip our direction.

Piper is the first to move. "You must be Ryan." We shake hands. "It's so nice to finally meet you. And

Ari?" She crouches down at eye level and waves. "I'm Piper."

Ari leans into my legs. "Hi. This is Shirley." She holds up her Velveteen Rabbit.

Piper grins, shaking the little rabbit's fingerless hand. "Nice to meet you both." She shoots a glance at Jake. "My little sister had a rabbit just like that." She smiles down at Ari. "I think we're taking off in about ten minutes, so you have some time. The bathroom is right through that door and to the left."

Ari looks up at me. "Will you come too?"

"Of course. It's nice to meet you all." I give an awkward half wave to Piper and Oliver, whose boiling glower has mellowed to a simmering scowl.

Probably best to let them talk without an audience. Thank god for little bladders.

The other room is a bedroom. A very plush, luxurious bedroom, with a queen-size bed covered in a dark-red comforter.

I glance through the door that leads into the bathroom and my eyebrows hit my hairline.

"Holy . . . this is huge."

Ari peers around, her brow furrowed. "It's not that big."

I press my lips together to hold back the laughter. "Most planes have bathrooms barely large enough to sit in."

"Hmm." She remains unconvinced. Wait till she has to fly coach.

It's almost as big as our master bath at home. There's a full-size shower and tub, all sparkling clean and gleaming white.

"Don't touch anything." I frown at the countertop. Is that marble?

"Momma, I have to touch things to go potty and wash my hands."

"Just be careful. I'll be right outside the door."

She takes her sweet time. The hum of the engine drowns most of the conversation happening in the other room. Only the tones are audible: Jake's baritone, Piper's higher pitch, and Oliver's occasional bark.

By the time we join the others, everyone has settled in their seats. We prepared Ari for what to expect with takeoff and whatnot, and she sits on the couch between Jake and me, her eyes wide as the plane lifts into the sky.

Oliver sits at one of the window seats across the plane from us, clicking away on a laptop.

Piper occupies the chair across from the couch. She points over to the front of the plane. "We have drinks and snacks in the fridge up there. If you want anything, please help yourself. There are also some premade sandwiches, apple slices, all kinds of stuff."

Jake gets up and grabs a few waters, along with animal crackers and apples for Ari.

We make small talk with Piper, and after a few minutes, Ari gets bored and takes her snacks over to a window seat behind Oliver to gaze out at the world below.

Jake nudges me with his shoulder, nodding toward Ari. "I'm surprised she hasn't wanted a nap."

"Does she normally nap?" Piper asks.

"Not usually, but she was up late because she was too excited to sleep."

Jake nods. "And then we had to wake up her early today to get to the airport."

Our gazes connect, and one corner of his mouth ticks up. Warmth spreads through my belly.

I snap my attention back to Piper.

Her eyes flick between the two of us.

Is it that obvious I want to bone her brother?

I clear my throat. "She's really excited the camp is named after her. We explained it was named for your sister, and she knows she was named after the same person, so we let her believe it."

Piper laughs. "I mean, she's not wrong."

Ari moves from her chair over to the one next to Oliver.

He scowls at her.

I wince. "I hope she isn't bothering him."

Piper twists around to check them out, and when she turns back, she's smiling. "He loves kids and for some reason, even though he can be a little prickly, they love him too."

Across the plane, Oliver has moved the desk forward so Ari can climb into his chair with him. She points at something on his computer screen.

I am sure she's asking something like, *Why?*

Piper asks more questions about Ari and Mia, and then the conversation turns to caring for a newborn.

Jake gets up to raid more food from the fridge.

"Honestly, I got pretty lucky," I tell Piper. "Ari woke up a couple times a night for the first nine months, but it was consistent, you know? I got used to it. I've heard horror stories about colic and newborns who were basically allergic to more than an hour of sleep at a time."

"It must be terrifying. Caring for a newborn."

"I guess, but you know, you just do it."

Piper rests her hand on her stomach.

Huh. Kind of like Sam when she— "Oh. You're . . ."

She glances over at Jake and then leans in toward me and lowers her voice. "We haven't told anyone yet. We're waiting until I'm a little farther along."

"I promise not to say a word."

"Thank you. Oliver is a little freaked. He lost his parents fairly young and had a hard time in foster families. He's scared of being a bad father."

We both glance over at him. Ari is asleep, leaning into Oliver, her face squished into his suit coat. His head is leaning back against the seat, his eyes closed.

"I am so sorry. She never does this, and to a complete stranger no less."

Piper's face softens, watching them.

"Something tells me he's going to do just fine."

By the time the plane lands, it's nearly six because of the five-hour flight plus the three-hour time difference. But we are able to land right on camp property because Oliver had a private airstrip built for his personal use, complete with hangar and fueling station.

We disembark and head toward a black Cadillac SUV parked about a hundred yards away. Standing outside the vehicle is an extremely broad, dark-haired man in a Camp Aria T-shirt and jeans, a wicked-looking scar bisecting his brow.

"That's Archer," Jake tells me as we approach.

He greets everyone with a hug, and an extra smack on the back for Jake.

"Damn, bro, easy on the violent affection."

Archer points at him. "You ever leave like that without word to Finley and I want you to remember, we have a lot of property and I learned how to operate some serious digging equipment when we were renovating the camp."

Jake sighs. "I know, man, I know. This is Ryan and Ari." He gestures to us.

"Hey." Archer smiles. "It's really nice to meet you both. Let me help you with your bags."

The back of the SUV is quickly loaded up with luggage and then we pile in, Oliver in the front seat, Piper, Jake, Ari, and me in the back.

We drive off the runway and onto a dirt road.

"There is pizza up at the main house if anyone's hungry," Archer says.

"I'm hungry," Ari pipes up.

"Great," Archer says. "I know Finley put some snacks and breakfast items in your cabin, but I'm not sure if there's enough in there to prepare a full meal or anything."

Piper chuckles. "That's probably part of her plan to get you all up to the main house for meals as frequently as possible."

"She loves to feed people, that's for sure," Archer adds.

"Is that a lake?" Ari points out the window.

"More of a pond," Jake says. "We can go fishing there though."

"I've never been fishing."

"I'll teach you."

Ari glances toward the front of the car. "Is Oliver going to come?"

Jake waves a hand. "We don't want him to be there."

Ari frowns. "Why not?"

"He's too good at everything."

"Then he should teach me."

Oliver turns around, a smile lighting his normally stern expression. "Kid's a genius."

Ari beams at him.

Jake rolls his eyes dramatically.

We travel up and over a hill, then the camp comes into view.

Brightly painted, stout wood cabins are scattered beneath looming pines. The dirt road transitions to cobblestone, rumbling underneath us and winding between the bungalows.

Ari is silent, staring out the window.

Archer turns the car uphill, and a few seconds later we park in front of a house next to a Jeep with the camp logo painted on the side.

"Wait. Are Taylor and Atticus here too?"

Archer shrugs. "Of course."

"Is that Luke's car? Is everyone here?" Jake asks. "Don't they have work or lives or something?"

"Guess not." Piper shrugs.

Ari stares up at the house looming outside the car window. "*What* is this place?"

Everyone chuckles. Even Oliver.

Oliver pushes open his door. "It's a monstrosity, I know, but they've done a lot of work on the interior so it's not terrible."

We all exit the car and I look up at the house, shading my eyes from the sun. Jake's childhood home. It's not a monstrosity by any means, but the large, two-story structure is an odd mixture of materials, dark wood, red brick, and a splash of stucco. It reminds me of when Ari built a house using a combination of Legos, popsicle sticks, and Play-Doh, but sturdier.

A woman stands on the porch, greeting us as we approach, hugging everyone as they pass, including me.

Jake introduces us.

"Ryan, it's so nice to meet you finally." Finley pulls me into a hug. She has the same dark hair as Jake and

Piper, her nose is slightly smaller, her lips fuller, but the family resemblance is uncanny.

"Thank you for having us."

"Are you kidding? I'm ecstatic." She loops her arm in mine, leading me inside. "Leave the bags in the car and then after dinner, Jake can take you to your cabin."

I glance behind us to check on Ari, but she's walking in with Jake, completely distracted by our surroundings.

Finley leads me through the front door, which opens into an office. I get a quick glimpse of two cluttered desks, walls of beige and pale blue, and then we're going through a connecting door.

"We've put you in one of our best cabins," Finley tells me. "Two bedrooms, a full-size kitchen already set up with the basics, and two full baths—the master suite has an attached bath. I also put one of our white noise machines in the second bedroom for Ari, just in case. Some kids have a hard time sleeping because it's so quiet. Ari's room has a bunk bed too. Jake mentioned she was excited about the prospect of sleeping in one."

The door from the office takes us into an open-concept living and dining space. A massive oak table takes up the bulk of the dining area, pizza boxes stacked on one side next to a salad bowl, along with some plates and utensils.

Four people are in the living room, sitting on the plush sofa and recliner. Their chatting comes to a halt as we enter.

I'm about to thank Finley for everything, but I don't

get a chance. The next few minutes are a rush of introductions: Taylor and her boyfriend Atticus, and Mindy and Luke Fletcher—I know who he is, of course, I've listened to his music plenty of times.

When he shakes my hand, I can't even speak, I just nod and flush. I've never met a famous musician. Or a famous anything. Now I've met three moderately famous people all in the same day.

After introductions, the commotion continues as everyone gets a plate of food and finds a place to sit, some around the dining table and a few in the living room.

I end up at the table with Jake's sisters and Luke, and Ari ends up in the living room with Jake, Atticus, and Archer.

"She's six, right?" Mindy asks, her eyes trained on where Ari is sitting on the couch next to Jake.

Archer is in the recliner next to them. He throws back his head and laughs, and Jake shakes his head, smiling down at Ari and then leaning closer to her to tell her something.

My bones ache with how sweet he is with her. She's so comfortable with him. Maybe I should be worried about her getting too attached, but I'm right there with her.

Finley picks at her salad with a fork. "Six is a great age. Young enough that they're still affectionate and old enough to wipe their own butts."

I laugh. "Do you have kids?"

"No. I work with campers of all ages who come here

though. We have counselors and scientists and whatnot that do all the instructing and most of the monitoring and interacting, but I like to be involved."

"She's amazing with kids," Piper interjects.

Finley shrugs her off. "Taylor, how's the plans for the next festival coming along?"

Taylor and Mindy chat about their Outfoxed Festival, a yearly event they put on every summer.

They give me the lowdown, expanding on the music, the art, the lights and campgrounds they set up for the event. I wish I could see it, but Ari and I will be long gone by then.

I keep half of my awareness on Ari, a habit that's impossible to break when you have a small child. When she finishes eating, Jake takes her to the kitchen to wash off her hands and face.

"Did you get pie?" he calls out from the other room.

"There's no pie in there," Finley yells back.

He appears in the doorway, clutching his chest. "Why hast thou forsaken me?"

Atticus grabs a slice of pizza from one of the boxes at the end of the table, setting it on his plate. "After all the times you tricked me into bringing you pie, I think you owe it to us to bring one over."

"Fine. I can get one tomorrow, but that doesn't help us now."

Archer rolls his eyes. "There's pie in the fridge out in the garage, you . . ." His eyes drop to Ari. "Meanie head."

"Slick burn. C'mon, superhero, let's go get dessert."

They disappear back into the kitchen. Distantly, a door opens and shuts.

Finley reaches over and puts her hand on my arm. "I know this might be a bizarre situation we're in, but I am truly happy you decided to come stay for a few days. If you need anything at all, please don't hesitate to ask. Honestly, it's like we're family."

"Thank you. It is weird, but it's also kind of not, if that makes sense?"

She leans back with a chuckle. "It does make sense, in a strange way."

It's like when I met Jake. What's weird is that it's not uncomfortable or awkward. Maybe it's because of Aria and that connection between our families. Maybe it's because they are such a welcoming group. I only had Mia and Mom for most of my life, so I'm not used to a large, rowdy family.

"It's pie time, the most wonderful time of the year." Jake appears in the doorway, a pie box in his hands while Ari is on his back, laughing and having a grand time.

"Pie for dinner and pie for dessert," Archer says.

Jake groans, setting the pie on the table. "For the last time, pizza is not a pie, just like a hot dog is not a sandwich."

"Not this again," Finley says under her breath, right as the whole table explodes into loud and rambunctious debate.

Chapter Nineteen

JAKE

Mindy rests a hand on Taylor's shoulder. "She's right, Jake. There's even a song. Something about the moon hitting your eye like a big pizza pie, or whatever."

Ugh. They're ganging up on me now. I shake my head in disgust. "I miss when you two hated each other. Family dinner just isn't the same."

Taylor lifts her brows. "Are you saying you enjoyed it when we would start yelling at each other randomly?"

"Yes. Someone would start a fight, people would stomp off, and then someone else could eat their feelings by devouring the food left behind."

Archer, standing at the head of the table cutting up the grape pie, hands Ryan a slice. "It's Jake. He was the one eating all the food left behind."

I cross my arms over my chest and shrug. "I don't believe in food waste."

"How very noble of you," Piper says drily.

"I think so."

We laugh and talk and eat the pie. Every time I glance over at Ryan, she and Finley are leaning close, chatting with each other. Ari is in my lap, her mouth smeared with fruit from the pie.

The whole scene spreads contentment through my bones. I've always loved time with my family, chatting, debating, and laughing with them, but it's like Ryan and Ari's presence adds an extra layer of satisfaction.

Once the pie has been demolished, Taylor, Atticus, Mindy, and Luke all bail for the night. They have work in the morning because of the upcoming festival, and Mindy and Luke are staying with them at their place, on the other side of town.

With their departure, the volume in the room cuts in half.

Ari yanks on my hand, jumping up and down. "What are we doing now?"

Ryan winces. "I'm afraid after the nap on the plane and all that sugar in the pie, someone is a little hyper."

I shrug. "It's only about six back in Dull."

"True."

Archer grabs a stack of dirty plates and cups, heading toward the kitchen. "You can take her down to firepit one. We have glow-in-the-dark ring toss and one of those giant-sized Connect Four games."

"Yes!" Ari shouts, the hopping growing more enthusiastic.

We pile into a couple of golf carts parked on the side of the house, Ari, Ryan, Piper, and me in one, and Archer, Finley and Oliver in another, and drive down into camp to the main firepit.

Archer lights the fire, and Piper and Finley pull out the games.

After about an hour of ring toss and Connect Four, her boundless energy finally starts to ebb.

Piper and Oliver head back to their cabin to turn in for the night, and the rest of us settle around the fire.

Ari sits between Ryan and me on one of the long benches, while Finley and Archer tell us about some of the recent happenings with the camp.

When there is a lull in the conversation, Ari speaks up. "Do you have any campfire stories?"

Finley grins at me from across the fire, the flames making her eyes glitter. "Remember Squinty Pete?"

A bark of laughter bursts from my throat. How had I forgotten? The memory rushes back, the first time Dad told us about Squinty Pete. We couldn't have been more than seven or eight. We had been helping him with some routine maintenance issues, Aria and I. More like following him around and annoying him, and then running around playing in the trees while he was working in the cabins.

"Don't go too far," he would tell us. "Squinty Pete might be out there."

It was his way of keeping us from wandering too far.

"Squinty Pete lives deep in the trees," I tell Ari now. "And he only has one eye, but it's a giant eye."

Her nose wrinkles. "One giant eye?"

"Yep," Finley says. "And he watches from the trees, waiting for little children to go deep enough into the forest and close enough for him to snatch."

I squeeze Ari's side, making her giggle.

"At night," Finley continues, "Squinty Pete comes out and looks for any candy or food little kids have left out to gobble up."

I chuckle. One of the clever ways Dad came up with to get us to throw away our trash without him having to ask over and over.

We share more camp stories, until Ari starts yawning and crawls into my lap, laying her head on my shoulder.

We make plans to all meet up for a tour of the camp after breakfast the next morning, and then I drive Ari and Ryan to their cabin.

I help them carry the bags inside. Ari races from room to room, excited about everything, from the kitchen already stocked with her favorite snacks to the bunk beds in her room and the flat-screen TV on the wall in the living room.

"Can I sleep on the top bunk?" she yells.

Ryan lifts her brow at me.

"There's a wood railing."

"Sure, honey," she calls out.

Ari's excited shriek is the only response.

We grin at each other.

Ryan glances around the kitchen. "This is really nice. Your family is . . ."

"Annoying? Pushy? Overbearing?"

She shakes her head. "Try amazing."

I make a face. "Yeah, I know."

Ari comes running out from her bedroom. "Jake, can you read me a bedtime story?"

"Of course."

"We have to at least wash up and brush your teeth first." Ryan leads her toward the bathroom, throwing me a glance over her shoulder. "Will you grab Shirley and the book from my bag? It's on the bed."

"Of course." I cross the living room into the master bedroom, easily locating her bag, opened on the bed. I move a sweater to the side and my hands still over an unopened box of condoms.

My heart picks up speed. My mouth goes dry. My cock is immediately at half-mast.

Did she want me to find this?

I swallow, hard. I have to pull myself together and read Ari a story.

After taking a few deep breaths, I locate Shirley and *The Velveteen Rabbit* and make my way back across the living room to the bathroom by Ari's room.

I stop outside the door, leaning against the wall. Ari is brushing her teeth while Ryan sings "Shake It Off" and they both shake their limbs, Ari giggling around her toothbrush.

My heart swells.

I have to convince Ryan to stay. What does she need to go back to Dull for? She hates it there. Her mother is gone, which is terrible, but true. She could live here, go back to school, work . . . anywhere, really. She wouldn't have to worry about care for Ari—we have a damn village already in place—and every person here would bend over backward to help with anything she needs.

Did she bring those condoms because she's hoping for the same thing I am? That we can find a way to be together?

They finish up in the bathroom, and I follow them into Ari's room still holding Shirley and the book.

Ryan climbs up on the ladder to give Ari a kiss. Then she hops down and walks over to me.

"I'm going to get myself ready for bed while you read to her, if that's okay?"

I hold the rabbit up in front of my face. "*Shirley* that's a rhetorical question because of course."

Ari giggles.

Ryan smacks me lightly on the shoulder. "Funny. And thank you."

I clamber up the ladder and squeeze in next to Ari, the bed only squeaking slightly in protest. She hugs Shirley to her chest while I read the book, adding as many ridiculous voices as I can, making Nana's voice deep and masculine, and giving the Boy the best British accent I can muster.

Ari giggles so hard she gets the hiccups.

We finish the story and despite my entertaining performance, her lids are already drooping. I kiss her forehead good night before climbing back down the steps and shutting off the light, leaving her door halfway open.

Out in the living room, Ryan is sitting on the chair in the corner, gazing out the window into the dark night.

"Hey. She's out."

She pushes herself to her feet, walking toward me.

"She seems pretty exhausted. I don't think there will be any waking up wanting wat—"

She reaches up, grabs my shoulders, and presses her mouth to mine, hard and quick, and then pulls back and searches my eyes. "Is this okay?"

I lick my lips. "It's more than okay. But are you sure?"

In response, she takes my hand, leading me to her bedroom, thankfully located on the opposite side of the cabin from Ari's room.

"What about Ari?"

"She's a deep sleeper once she's out." She shuts her bedroom door behind us, turning to face me. "But try not to scream."

I chuckle, but then she whips her shirt over her head and the laughter dies in my throat.

We're less than a foot apart. There's a lamp behind me somewhere, casting a soft, buttery glow over every dip and curve. My mouth goes dry.

She reaches for the snaps on her bra, and I stop her,

resting my fingers on her hand. "Wait." I swallow. "I don't want to rush this." I haven't done this in so long, and never with someone I care about this much. I'm suddenly terrified I'll screw it up somehow. "I want to unwrap you myself."

And I want to make sure she experiences as much pleasure as possible before I take my own, because my cock is already throbbing against my zipper in time with the drumming of my heart.

I reach out, cupping her face in my hands and dipping my head to hers.

Our lips meet, mesh, move together.

Her hands grip my shoulders.

I brush my tongue against hers, over and over, until the pads of her fingers are digging into me and she's gasping into my mouth.

Pulling back, I reach behind me to pull my shirt up and over my head, then we're kissing again, the silky fabric of her bra rubbing against my bare chest and setting every nerve ending aflame.

Our mouths go from sweet, to sensual, to straight-up erotic. A tidal wave of desire sweeps over me. I lift her into my arms, turning us toward the bed and laying her down before coming over top of her, kissing along her jawline and then down her chest.

I brush my lips over the smooth material, gently sucking.

She arches underneath me, her breath coming out in pants.

"Jake."

I keep moving, kissing over the soft skin of her belly to the top of her jeans. I fumble with the button, flicking it open and then unzipping to wiggle them down her thighs and off, chucking them over the side of the bed.

I slide my hands up her thighs, spreading them wide enough for me to settle in between.

Her fingers grasp and twist the bedspread underneath her.

She still has her panties on. Just a tantalizing swath of black cotton.

Nerves coil in my gut. It's been so long. What if I suck at this? "I haven't done this in a while, so . . ."

Heart pounding, I smooth my fingers up and down over her panties.

"Oh, yes," she moans.

Well, she likes that.

"Show me." I take her hand, moving it between her legs. "Show me what you like."

Her fingers move. Lust squeezes me in a vise. Only two of my brain cells are functioning, and they're both too horny to think clearly, but I bang them together a few times and focus on Ryan's movements, paying attention to the places she touches, how she touches, the motions and the force behind them.

After a few minutes of careful study, I take over. The undies get yanked off and thrown on the floor with the pants, and then I use my mouth and hands and fingers.

I don't stop until Ryan is trembling and shaking

underneath my mouth, smothering her groans with one hand as release overtakes her.

I kiss my way back up her body and collapse next to her on the bed.

"Holy shit," she breathes. "For someone who hasn't done this in a while, you did a stellar job. Gold star."

I grin up at the ceiling. I don't suck. Awesome.

She rolls into me, kissing my shoulder, her hand running down my stomach to the top of my jeans.

She smirks at me, her eyes drowsy, and shoves at my pants.

I clench my jaw. She must be exhausted from traveling all day, plus staying up late playing games with Ari. "We can stop now if you want," I murmur.

She stops pushing at my clothes and blinks at me. "What?"

"If you're tired, we can just sleep."

She shakes her head. "No. We're doing this. I am not too tired for this."

Thank Christ.

"Here, let me help you." I shuck my jeans off, then we both fumble with her bra, and then we're kissing again, limbs tangling.

"Condom," she says, rolling away from me to reach into her bag on the floor by the bed.

The wrapping crinkles as she rips it open, then together we slide it on. The grip of her hand around my length shoots stars across my vision. Before I can make any other moves, she swings a leg over my hip and slides down.

My eyes are trained on the place where we're joining as I disappear inside her.

We both moan.

Pure bliss. Rapture. Ecstasy.

Oh yeah. This is not lasting long.

She moves over me, riding me, and the whole world evaporates. It's only me and Ryan and this moment. I cup her breasts in my hands, flicking the tips with my thumbs.

She throws her head back and moves faster.

I thrust my hips upward in time with her movements, focusing all my energy on not spending.

It's brutal. The orgasm builds and builds, ready to burst through me like a geyser about to blow.

Not yet, not yet, not yet is a mantra beating in my veins until I can't take it any longer.

My spine tingles. My balls tighten.

The release overpowers me, reverberating through me, stealing the breath from my lungs and crowding my vision with black spots.

I grip Ryan's thighs, my eyesight returning just in time to witness her quaking and shuddering as she comes.

She collapses on top of me, sticky and sweaty and so goddamn perfect I'm about out of my mind with emotions too immense and fragile to put a name to.

We lie there, breathing together for a few long

minutes, until she pushes herself up slightly to meet my eyes.

"Shower?"

"Hell yeah."

We rinse off, making each other slippery with the soap, which leads to another orgasm each using fingers and hands and it's the best shower I've ever had in my life.

After toweling off, we fall into bed, folding into each other perfectly. Like peanut butter and jelly, or mustard and hot dogs, or cheese and . . . more cheese.

I brush a kiss to her forehead. "I'll get up in a little bit and go back to the house before morning. Before Finley notices I'm gone, or Ari realizes I'm here."

She nods, tucking her head into my neck. "Mmmkay."

I'm going to shut my eyes, just for a minute.

"Momma!"

The shriek jerks me awake.

The sun is shining through the blinds.

It's . . . daytime?

"Can we have pancakes for breakfast?"

My head rolls toward the door.

Standing in the open doorway is Ari. Her eyes are wide. "Jake? What are you doing here? Did you have a sleepover?"

Chapter Twenty

Jake

Pull yourself together, man.

"Um, yep, that's it, just a regular, run-of-the-mill sleepover. As we do. You know, grown-ups, kids, we all like sleepovers."

Ryan has burrowed down, under the blankets, out of sight, her limbs trembling against mine.

Is she laughing?

Ari is still watching me, a divot between her brows and a frown marring her face.

I pull the sheet up a little, even though it's already over most of my chest. "Why don't you go find the pancake mix in one of the cabinets? I think it's in the bottom one by the stove. I'll be right there. "

"Okay."

Ari disappears, leaving the door wide open. A second later, a cabinet door slams.

I yank the blanket off of Ryan's head. "Are you laughing?"

She covers her mouth with a hand, giggles bubbling up around it. "I'm sorry. This isn't funny. Do you think she's traumatized?"

"No, but I think I am."

That just makes her laugh harder.

I rub her shaking back. "This is my fault. I meant to sneak out before she woke up."

Her hand comes up to pat my cheek. "It's okay. I totally wore you out. Not your fault."

I chuckle. "Yes, you did."

"I'm hoping to do it again in, say, twelve hours?"

I groan. "So far away. Maybe I can trick Finley into watching Ari for a few hours."

"No, we can't do that."

"Are you kidding me? She would love it."

Ryan smiles. I take in her sleepy eyes, creamy skin, mussed hair. My half-mast rises to a full mast.

Pancakes. Ari. Focus.

I swallow and roll out of bed. Distance is the only way to rein in the lust.

"I've got this." We need to talk, but it will have to wait. After last night, I'm even more hell-bent on convincing her to stay. This weekend can't be the end of . . . whatever this is. I grab my jeans from the ground and tug them up my waist. "For now, what do you want me to tell her?"

I turn around.

She's watching me with heavy-lidded eyes, biting her lip. Her eyes jerk up to my face and she flushes.

I grin, euphoria flooding through my veins. She's as lusty as I am right now, and it's awesome.

She scrubs a hand down her face. "As little as possible."

I slip my T-shirt over my head and then bend over to brush a kiss against her bare shoulder. "Take your time. Take a shower, get ready, whatever you want. I've got breakfast."

She blinks. "Really?"

"Of course."

Her smile widens. "Okay."

I give her one last kiss on the lips, a quick one because morning breath, and then she disappears into the bathroom. I head out to the kitchen.

"Who wants my world-famous pancakes?"

"Me me me!"

We eat pancakes and bacon and then I head up to the main house. I need a shower and fresh clothes. It's going to be a busy day.

Finley accosts me as soon as I walk in the side door, into the kitchen.

"Well, well, well." She leans against the counter next to Archer, lifting a bright red mug to her lips and taking a quick sip. "Enjoying an early morning walk, Jacob?"

I scrub a hand through my messy hair. "Yep."

"Hey, isn't that what you were wearing yesterday?" Archer lifts his brows.

"Nope. You must be mistaken. I was wearing a green shirt yesterday. So anyway, gotta shower." I bolt out of the kitchen so fast I think I leave track marks, but not quick enough to escape the laughter chasing me out of the room.

Thankfully, when I come back downstairs, Finley is all business and I'm not subjected to any questioning under a hot lamp.

When Finley has an objective with a time limit, she turns into a hyperactive, overly methodical tyrant. Like a border collie, but with spreadsheets.

We leave Archer behind to get some work done—Finley has been overwhelmed with paperwork on camp business—and we take one of the golf carts down the hill to pick up our guests. Finley insists on driving as she's the one with the plan.

Ari climbs into the passenger seat next to Finley, and Ryan hops into the rear-facing seat in the back of the cart, next to me.

Our hips brush, heat blooming at the point of contact and spreading through the rest of my body.

My cock jerks.

Holy hell.

She tucks her hair behind her ear. "Hey."

I swallow and take a slow breath, willing my body to calm down. I can't seriously be so horny right now.

"Hi." The greeting is more of a croak than an actual word. I want to kiss her. I want to yank her against me, run my hands down her back, cup her ass, I didn't get nearly enough contact time with her body—

Finley twists in the front seat to greet Ryan, cutting off any more lustful thoughts.

"Hey, Ryan. I hope you slept well."

I don't have to look at Finley to know she's smirking.

If she embarrasses me, I swear I will . . . probably do nothing at all. I clench my teeth.

"I slept great, thanks."

"We have a full schedule today. Are you ready, Ari?"

"I'm ready!"

"Wooo!"

And then we're off.

Finley keeps Ari entertained as we complete a loop around the camp, giving a whole speech on every building we pass and everything the camp has to offer from the art building to the paintball course to the indoor ice rink.

"I've never ice-skated," Ari says after we've passed the giant barnlike structure.

"We will definitely have to fix that," Finley tells her.

Then we stop at the mess hall for a few snacks and to use the bathrooms.

"This is incredible," Ryan says when Finley points out the restaurant-grade kitchen connected to the mess hall. It's used for meal preparation, and there are also stations where the kids are taught how to cook and prep their own food.

After the kitchens, we tour the perimeter of the property, and Finley lets Ari steer the cart along the well-worn dirt roads. We stop a few times for short nature walks—there are tons of wooded areas to explore—and then we head over the hill to the pond for a picnic. Archer meets us there, bearing a giant picnic basket and a few large blankets.

"What part did you like the best?" Finley hands Ari a turkey sandwich.

We've all spread out on blankets in the shade of one of the many sprawling trees surrounding the pond.

Ari taps her chin with her finger. "I liked the art place."

Everyone loves the art building. It has space for pottery, welding supplies and junk for metalwork, and anything anyone could ever need for painting, drawing, and sculpting.

"But," Ari continues, "I really want to ice-skate."

Finley beams at Ryan, then me. "I knew I liked this girl. What do you say we head over there after lunch? I can show you the basics. Once you learn how to fly on the ice, it's the most amazing feeling in the world."

"Finley is the best person to teach you," I tell Ari. "She could have been in the Olympics."

If tragedy hadn't struck.

"Really?" Ryan's eyes lift to her hairline. "That's incredible. What happened?"

Finley stands up, wiping her hands on her jeans. "Life got in the way. As it does."

Ryan frowns. "Yeah. I've had that kind of thing happen too."

She placed first in sectionals a week before Aria died. She dropped everything and came home to take care of us. She gave up all her dreams.

Finley watches me like she can read the thoughts tumbling in my head. I clear my throat and crumple up the bag of chips I just demolished. "Did you bring dessert?" I ask Archer.

We spend a couple of hours at the ice rink, goofing around and burning off lunch.

Then Luke, Atticus, and Oliver meet us at the paintball course for a round before we all head to Veronica's to meet the rest of my family for dinner.

Taylor owns Veronica's, but she kept the old name. Veronica was an old friend of our dad's. We hung out in the bar all the time when we were kids. We'd eat all the cherries and orange slices, help her sweep the floors, and dust the bar. It's like a home away from home.

A place where I used to go to get smashed. Being here doesn't make me want to drink, but it does make me a little sad about all the time I wasted disappearing instead of living. Although I suppose I had to make those mistakes to get to where I am now.

By the time we finish eating and head back to the cabins, it's late and Ari's eyes are drooping.

Archer drops Ryan and Ari off at their place first before heading back to the main house.

"Did you want to get out here too?" Archer winks at me after Ryan and Ari have exited the vehicle.

I don't want to make Ryan uncomfortable by assuming, and he knows it, the prick.

We head back home, Finley and Archer disappear upstairs—as they often do—and I'm sitting on the couch in the living room staring at Ryan's number, wondering if I should call her, when the little chat bubbles appear on the screen. Then my phone pings with an incoming text.

I can't find Shirley.

I frown and hit the call button.

Ryan answers on the first ring. "She can't sleep without it. I think today was a little too exciting and now she's so tired she's almost hyper."

"It's not in Ari's bunk bed somewhere? She had it last night."

She sighs. "No. We looked in there, under all the blankets on the top and bottom bunk, plus underneath the whole thing. I'm sure it's here somewhere, I just have no idea where."

Ari's voice escalates in the background. "Mommaaaa."

Ryan sighs. "I'm sorry to bother you. I can take care of this. She's being stubborn."

"Um, listen, we might have another Velveteen Rabbit here. It's older and dustier, but I'll bring it over if I can find it. Gimme a couple minutes and I'll let you know."

We hang up and I lift my gaze toward her room on the second floor, as if I can see through the walls into the space. I haven't gone in Aria's room since she died. I always knew part of my recovery would mean confronting the remnants of her life, everything she left behind, the room she occupied, decorated, and made her own.

Trudging up the stairs, my feet are like cement blocks. Each step clangs louder and louder.

My hands are shaking. This sucks. My therapist would be so proud of me right now though.

I stop at the top of the stairs. Faint illumination paints the floor of the hallway in a buttery glow. It's coming from a Minnie Mouse nightlight, plugged into the wall by the bathroom door. I stare at the faded Disney character. It was Aria's. When we were five, she insisted on moving it from her room to the hallway because I was scared of the dark. It probably hasn't been touched since.

I can do this, for Ari. And for myself.

Pushing open the door, I flick on the light.

A lamp in the corner brightens to life, casting a faded

glow over the musty room. The Velveteen Rabbit is still here, sitting on her pillow.

I stare at it. I just need to grab it and leave.

But I can't move.

The world comes to a screeching halt.

Memories engulf me, running through my mind like a movie on fast-forward. Childhood laughter and games, playing with dolls and having tea parties, which I pretended to hate but truly didn't mind one bit. The tears and drama and struggles of middle school, of new friends and fights and first crushes.

All of it, cut short too soon. Before she really had a chance to experience life.

I walk inside, taking a few steps before my legs give out, and I drop to a seat on the bed, running my fingers over the black and white bedspread.

Around freshman year, Aria decided she liked dark colors. Really, anything but pink. Her whole room transformed from Barbies and pastels to dark purples and blacks and pops of yellow.

I'm surprised there isn't an inch of dirt over everything.

Finley's probably been keeping it clean.

My gaze snags on a photo on the dresser of Aria with her best friend from school, Willow. Their arms are around each other, heads pressed together, bright smiles on both of their faces.

I saw Willow a couple years ago. Her parents own the

hardware store in town. She wanted to meet up for coffee or dinner, to chat.

To chat about Aria.

I made up some lame excuse to avoid it, as one does.

My eyes trail over other relics from the past, a paperweight that Piper fashioned in the shape of a golden retriever and then painted in gold. Prince. The dog from *The 10th Kingdom*. Aria loved animals. Any animals. All animals.

Including one Velveteen Rabbit. I reach over and pluck it off the pillow, resting it in my lap and rubbing at the ear, softened with age and time.

Footsteps sound down the hall and then stop.

I look up.

Archer is staring at me with his mouth open. "Uh, you all right?"

"Yeah. I needed to get this . . ." I look down at the stuffed animal in my hands. I can't see Ryan right now. I'm too raw. Too needy. "Will you bring this down to Ryan and Ari? They can't find hers."

"Sure, man. Absolutely." He crosses into the room, and I hand over the rabbit.

He hesitates in the doorway, tapping the frame with a finger, his mouth opening and then shutting, and then thankfully he stalks away.

I wasn't ready to come into this room, but now I'm not sure I'm ready to leave.

It hurts. But the pain has changed. I will never stop missing her. Ever. But something has shifted inside me since I found out about Aria's heart and Mia and little Ari. It's like . . . I'm still wrecked, but it's different. I still miss her more than life itself, but the sharp edge of pain has dulled into a blunt ache.

On the nightstand, there's another framed photo of our ultrasound picture. Just a bunch of blurry dots on a black background. Dad found it in an old box and Aria insisted on framing it.

I'm hurled back into the memory, Aria's wide, excited eyes, her laughing mouth as she held it up and proclaimed, "Our first photo!"

We came into this world together and I never wanted to be in it without her. She's always been a part of me. She will always be a part of me. It's unfathomable that she's gone.

The black and white image swims in front of my eyes, hot tears disappearing into the dark bedspread.

I swipe them away.

"Hey." Finley strides inside, her eyes wide and concerned. She perches next to me on the bed.

I set the photo back on the nightstand. "Did Archer make you come here?"

She puts an arm around me, her head pressing against my shoulder. "He didn't make me *do* anything. But he did look like he'd seen three ghosts, a demon, and a life-sized spider playing poker. He was seriously freaked."

I lean my head on hers. "You've been cleaning in here."

"Just dusting a bit here and there, yeah."

"Is it . . . hard for you? To come in here? See all this?"

"Yes, and no." She straightens. "Losing Aria was hard for all of us. But it was the worst for you."

I stare down at a yellow nail polish stain on the faded rug at my feet. "She was a part of me."

I don't know how else to describe it.

It can't be described.

"You always knew exactly where she was."

"What do you mean?"

"Like that time we went on a hike to Mayberry Falls, it was me you, Aria, and Dad and she wandered off. Remember?"

"No."

"I think you were about nine, maybe? Anyway, she went to pee but then never came back. We started yelling for her, going in the direction she had walked off, but then Dad just looked at you and said, 'Point to where she is.' You did, which was not the same direction she had gone to pee, but we found her a minute later. She had seen a deer and tried to follow it and got turned around and couldn't find her way back."

I search my memory banks and come up empty. "I don't remember that."

"Really?" She shifts to face me more fully. "You would do it all the time. We had to stop playing hide-and-seek if you were the seeker and she was hiding because you knew exactly where she would be. It was nuts. You did it one time in the grocery store when you were both maybe four or five."

I've forgotten. Did I lose the memories because I shy away from all thoughts of her? Refuse to think of her? Does that mean I will eventually lose all the memories, good and bad, because of my fear of confronting thoughts about her?

It's painful, but I don't want to forget everything.

"I could never tell her no."

Finley rubs my arm. "I know."

"No. You don't. I should have been the one driving, but she begged me to drive home. And I couldn't tell her no."

Jake, please. If you let me drive, I'll do your chores for a week. A month. I need to practice, it's late so there won't be other cars. It's a short drive. You'll be with me.

"Aria's death was not your fault."

I've heard this, over and over, from everyone, but they don't understand and I can't deal with the truth.

Because it was.

So many moments, decisions made, events burned into my memory, no matter how many times I try to forget them.

Lying on this exact bed with Aria while she begged me to go with her to some party she had overheard Taylor on the phone talking to a friend about.

I could never tell her no.

And then . . .

"There was a cat."

228

"What?"

"It ran in front of the car. We were going too fast. I encouraged her to go fast because it was late. I was worried someone would notice we were gone. The streets were empty. What was the harm?" My voice cracks on the word. "But there was harm."

"Oh, Jake." Her arms fly around me, gripping me tight.

I barely feel it. My limbs have gone numb.

"She didn't die right away."

Finley tenses against me. "What?"

"She was scared." The words are quiet, whispered.

I dream about it, sometimes, Aria's eyes before she died, wide with terror.

"If we hadn't gone to that party, she might still be alive. I didn't want to go, but Aria wanted to follow Taylor. I could have convinced her to stay home."

She squeezes my arm. "No. You couldn't have. She was so stubborn. The most willful of all of us, and that's saying something."

I need to let go of the pain and guilt I'm dragging with me everywhere I go. The weight is pulling me down and, worse, erasing all the good memories of Aria. She would hate this.

"Holy shit. Am I dreaming?" Taylor walks into the room.

"Only if it's some creepy shared hallucination." Mindy is right behind her.

Followed by Piper. "Definitely a group hallu-cination."

Finley shifts on the bed, tucking up her legs to make room. "Like that time you three saw that pterodactyl?"

Taylor plops next to her. "Now that was real."

Piper rounds the bed to sit on my other side. "It was a legit pterodactyl."

Finley chuckles. "Maybe it was the moth man."

"West Virginia is a bit far for him to fly." Mindy rests her hip against the wooden bed frame.

I twist my lips. "But the pterodactyl, a creature that existed sixty-seven million years ago, that's a possibility?"

Taylor reaches around Finley to shove me in the shoulder. "It makes sense, okay?"

Piper nods solemnly. "The government has been lying to us."

"Speaking of." Mindy narrows her gaze my way. "What's going on with you and Ryan?"

I lift my hands in question. "How does speaking of government lies lead you to question me about Ryan?"

"Just answer the question," Taylor chimes in.

I groan. "Why are you all here anyway?"

"We came to say goodbye. Luke and I are leaving in the morning."

Piper nods. "Same here. I have a show the day after tomorrow at the gallery."

"Stop avoiding the question." Mindy points at me.

I shake my head. "I am not having this conversation with all of you."

Finley grins. "I like her." She glances around at the rest of my sisters. "Jake didn't come home last night. He snuck back into the main house this morning."

"What's that now?" Taylor laughs. "Jake *clearly* likes her too."

I hate that my face is burning right now. "I fell asleep."

Finley bites her lip, holding back her mirth. "Like when I fell asleep with Archer that one time in the laundry room?"

I cover my face with both hands. "No. Please don't. Don't make me remember. I am still traumatized."

Piper leans her shoulder into me. "Or when I fell asleep with Oliver in the loft of that one cabin where the bed is visible from the front door, and we had just woken up and you waltzed right in and saw more than you bargained for."

Mindy makes a hmming sound. "That reminds me of when I was making Luke breakfast in my underwear that one time and you came in without knocking."

Taylor gasps. "Oh my God! Like when I was with Atticus in our tent during the festival last year."

"You know what the common denominator is here?" Finley crosses her arms over her chest.

I glance around. "You're all a bunch of sexual deviants?"

Mindy tsks. "You need to learn how to knock, Jacob."

They burst out laughing.

"I've also learned that, unlike my sisters, I should lock doors when I don't want to be interrupted."

"Wouldn't it be great if we could all walk in on him?" Piper laughs but then frowns.

"Eww." Taylor smacks her on the arm.

Mindy makes a gagging sound. "What, no? Are you kidding?"

Bursts of laughter echo around the room, while Piper tries to defend herself. "It's not my fault, I have baby brain."

The amusement abruptly cuts off, like a door slammed shut on the hilarity.

"Did you say . . . *baby* brain?"

Suddenly, everyone is in motion while talking over each other and squealing all at the same time, almost dogpiling on top of me to get to Piper. I think Taylor kicks me in the shin.

"I can't believe it."

"I'm so freaking happy for you!"

"I get to be an aunty!"

"Is Oliver pissing his pants?"

"How far along?"

I wait until they stop hugging her to get my own embrace in. They keep talking and I half listen, my mind spinning around Piper's news, around Aria's bedroom, about what I shared with Finley.

It's kind of funny how we were all impacted by Aria's death.

Piper disappeared into her art. She never came home

when Dad was sick. She couldn't handle being home at all.

Mindy became one with her career, losing herself in finding musicians and turning them into rock stars.

Taylor decided to roam around and party at musical festivals like the weirdo hippie she is.

Finley couldn't leave. She threw herself into the business, attempting to save our family property like that would somehow bring Aria back.

And that leaves me. I wanted to forget. I focused on Dad, and then after he passed, I focused on numbing myself, but there were no answers at the bottom of a whiskey bottle.

"Hey." Finley leans toward me, her voice low. "You okay?"

I glance at our sisters still talking avidly. It's strange, Piper is bringing in a new life while we're in here, a place memorialized since Aria's death.

"I don't know. But I think I will be."

Chapter Twenty-One

RYAN

I press my toes into the hardwood underneath me, pushing off and rocking the porch swing back and forth, gazing out into the night.

Archer brought over the Velveteen Rabbit over an hour ago. I immediately took it to Ari in her bunk bed, who clutched it to her chest and fell asleep almost instantly. The toy was old and worn, the fabric softened and gray with time. Was it Aria's old toy? Was that hard for Jake, to find and hand it over? I hope he's okay.

Fireflies flicker to life, appearing and disappearing near the tree line. The cobblestone street winding through the cabins and trees glows in the moonlight.

This place is pure magic.

It's partially the landscaping, the cabins, and twinkling lights. The whole layout is like stepping into an enchanted fairyland. The other magic is Jake's family.

I only had Mia growing up. Ari is the only family I have left.

Earlier today, when we were on the paintball course, Finley and I kept watch from the fence surrounding the course.

Archer had climbed up in a tree to implement a surprise attack on Jake, tagging him square in the back when he passed by underneath.

Jake released a high-pitched shriek, a sound I never thought possible emerging from him.

Luke jumped out from behind the shell of a building to take aim at Archer. "Ah ha! Revenge time!"

At which point Ari popped up out of a giant tire well and shot Luke in the chest.

Finley clapped. "Nice work!" she shouted and then turned to me. "It's too bad you won't be able to stay through next week. We're getting a group of campers around Ari's age."

"She would love that. I wish she had siblings." I wince. "I mean, not that I'm ready to have more kids or even in a relationship or a position to have any, but I had my sister, you know, and it was a special bond. I just wish Ari had something like that too."

"I get it. And hey, this might be weird, but feel free to consider us your surrogate siblings."

Except I do not want to think of Jake like a brother.

Finley continued, "And Ari can think of us as surrogate aunts and uncles. I'm sure one of us will be popping out a kid at some point. So . . . cousins?"

"Thank you. That's really nice, truly, you've been too kind. Inviting us out here, letting us stay and feeding us and," I gesture to the paintball course, where Ari is now chasing Oliver with her gun, "all of this."

She grins. "It is great, isn't it? Although, that reminds me." She glances at her watch. "I have to head back to the office. The amount of paperwork I have to complete on a daily basis is a nightmare. Even when we don't have kids on site, the admin tasks never end. I would much rather spend time here." She gestures to the rink. "But we're having some weird issue with our payroll software that I have to figure out by tomorrow to make sure everyone gets paid on time."

"Do you use XpressPay?"

It's what I use, a common payroll software. I had an issue the other week that took forever to fix, sitting on hold with the help line just to get the details on how to fix it.

"Yeah, that's what we use."

"I know exactly what the problem is. There's a work-around to get it to submit. You have to adjust the account settings, then log out and log back in. I had to do it last pay period."

"Can you show me?"

"Absolutely."

"You are an angel. That will save me so much time. I also have been meaning to return about a million calls from vendors for our wedding. You'll come, right? It's in September."

"Of course." Er. Maybe. Would it be weird? Where will Jake and I be at that point in our . . . relationship, if that's even what this is? What if it's just a fling, and I come back in the fall and he's with someone else?

I'm not sure my heart could take it. We haven't talked about if this thing between us means anything at all.

It feels like everything.

Headlights appear in the distance, growing closer.

I push to a stand and walk to the porch railing as the cart parks in front of the cabin.

Jake jumps out of the cart, jogging up the steps and stopping when we're at eye level.

"Hi." I glance down at my feet, a sudden wave of self-consciousness flowing over me.

"Hey." His hand lifts, threading through my hair and then his mouth brushes mine. "I'm so sorry I took too long. I got held up talking to my sisters." His eyes search mine, his fingers gently tugging at my hair. "I had to go into Aria's room for the Velveteen Rabbit and I haven't been in there since . . . since."

I lift my hand to cover his, squeezing his fingers. "Do you want to talk about it?"

His brows dip. "I don't know. My sisters were there, and we talked and it was good, but a bit overwhelming. I don't really know what to do with myself. I think I'm a little talked out."

I get it. I've experienced the emotional exhaustion. "Come on."

Linking our fingers, I draw him inside, through the front door, which he immediately locks behind us, and then through the living room and kitchen into the master bedroom.

The lights are off, the drapes pulled open, bathing the room in moonlight and shadows.

"Is it okay if I hold you?" I ask.

He nods, his expression unreadable in the darkness. He yanks his shirt over his head, then pushes his pants off. I'm already in my sleep shorts and tee. We climb into bed, reaching for each other. I throw a leg over his hip, and his arm takes the space underneath my head. I never want to stop touching him. He's all lean muscles and warm skin. He smells like soap and aftershave and an underlying hint of spice that's purely Jake.

I could breathe him in forever.

We lay entwined together, skin to skin, not moving or speaking for so long I start to doze off.

"I told Finley about the night Aria died."

His voice is deep and husky, and just loud enough to draw me from the edge of sleep.

I rub his back with my fingers. "That's good. Sharing the burdens makes the load lighter."

His arms flex around me. "I think you're right," he murmurs.

We spend the next day in Ithaca, a picturesque city surrounded by rolling hills and state parks. We take the hike to Buttermilk Falls, one of Mia's favorite places to visit during the summers.

She would sit on a flat rock with her feet in the water, watching people swim, wishing her heart had the strength to join them.

We eat lunch at the Boatyard Grill, watching rowers move down the Cayuga, and then head to the Cornell Botanical Gardens in the afternoon.

When Ari complains about her legs hurting from all the walking, Jake doesn't miss a beat. He crouches down so she can climb up onto his back.

We take the woodland walk along a trickling stream, and Jake points out some of the plants he knows, like the Japanese primrose, ferns, and azaleas.

"You know a lot about plants," Ari says.

"I blame Atticus," he tells her. "He's a botanist and he never shuts up about plants."

"This place is pretty." Ari rests her head on Jake's shoulder.

My heart melts.

"It is beautiful." Almost whimsical, really, the effusion of plants covering the ground surrounding the stream, the blanket of green highlighted by pops of red and pink and white flowers.

Since we have to be back in Whitby for dinner—it's our last night here, and Finley made plans for roasting

hot dogs and grilling burgers around one of the firepits—
we head back to the car after the short hike.

Ari falls asleep before we've even left the parking lot.

Jake glances at her in the rearview mirror. "Damn,
she's cute when she's sleeping. I mean, she's always cute,
but I hardly ever get to see her not in motion."

I twist around in the passenger seat. She's slumped in
her booster, head tilted at what has to be the most
uncomfortable angle ever, her mouth halfway open, the
new old Velveteen Rabbit clutched in her lap.

We still haven't found Shirley, but the new rabbit,
Wanda, as Ari has decided to name her, has been suffi-
cient, it seems.

Heading toward the freeway, we pass through part of
the Cornell University campus.

I could have gone here, walked these sidewalks to
class, and passed the McGraw Tower every day.

"Have you ever thought about coming back?
Applying again?" Jake asks.

It's like he's inside my mind. "I don't know. It's too
late now."

"It's never too late."

"There's no guarantee I would get in."

My heart thumps harder in my chest, my stomach
twisting. I'm scared. What am I so scared of? Leaving
Dull? I don't like living there. I only stayed because of
Mom. So, what's left for me now? Just Bernie, really.

Change is scary.

Jake is scary. No, it's not Jake, it's my feelings for Jake that are terrifying.

He clicks the blinker to make a left-hand turn. "I like you. A lot."

I stare at his profile. "I like you too."

The light turns green. His ears turn pink. "I don't want to pressure you, but I want to be in your life, yours and Ari's life."

I want the same thing, but . . . "We live on opposite sides of the country."

"I could move," he answers quickly.

"And leave your whole family? Your whole life here?"

He bites his lip. "You could move."

The fear whispers in my ear: What if he changes his mind? Shane did. Does he really mean it? Maybe he does, now, but what if he regrets it later? "I don't know."

His finger taps on the steering wheel. "I'm not ready to say goodbye forever."

We're leaving early tomorrow morning. "I'm not either."

He shoots me a surprised glance. "Really?"

"Really. Maybe we can come back sometime soon. Or you can come visit."

"When?"

"I don't know."

"Maybe in a few days?"

A laugh bubbles out of me. "Maybe slightly longer than that."

It's not only about trusting him with my heart, but Ari's too.

If I did uproot our lives and move across the country, and then Jake and I didn't work out? It would break both our hearts.

We arrive back at the camp, and time picks up like a snowball gathering speed down a steep mountain.

Before I know it, we've eaten our last dinner with Jake's family and said our goodbyes.

Finley hugs me tight. "Don't be a stranger."

I can't make any promises.

Jake comes back with us to the cabin to read Ari her bedtime story.

I stand outside the bedroom door, out of sight, while Jake inflects silly voices, ad-libs lines, and makes Ari giggle.

Is there anything more attractive than a man who loves my daughter? Who makes her laugh, puts her needs first, shows care and concern, and gives her genuine affection?

My heart aches, part tenderness, part loss.

"Hey." His eyes search my face.

"Hey."

His head tips to one side. "Are you all right?"

In answer, I take his hand, and lead him away from Ari's room, across the living room, into the master bedroom and shut the door.

"What are you—?"

Then I drop to my knees in front of him.

"*Holy hell.*"

I unbutton his jeans, tugging them down along with his boxers far enough to pull his length out.

"Ryan. You don't have to—"

I take him in my mouth.

He hisses out a breath, his hands clenching at his side. "Scratch that. Ignore me. Do as you will."

Oh, I will. He went as hard as stone as soon as I touched him. It's thrilling how I can affect him so easily, just as much as he can affect me.

I take him into my mouth. Licking, sucking, teasing with my tongue, my mouth, my hands, driving him to the brink and then drawing away.

He watches me, his mouth ajar, his eyes glittering in the low light, lust a palpable thing between us.

He reaches down, pulling me up. "I want to be inside you."

I want the same. More than anything.

Quietly, we undress. Clothing hits the floor, one piece of apparel at a time, until we're both naked and gazing at each other.

As if it's choreographed, we move at the same time. The moment our bare skin connects, we both gasp. His arms go around my waist, my hands grip his neck, fingers threading into his hair.

Our mouths connect, the kiss slow and deep. Every nerve ending in my body fires to life.

We get lost in each other, touching, savoring every

sensation for a few long minutes, until we fall down onto the bed together.

There is nothing as glorious as tangling my limbs with Jake, our mouths searching, fingers exploring, playing with each other until we're both delirious with desire.

I'm surrounded by a lust-fueled fog as he rolls on the condom and shifts back between my thighs. I wrap my legs around him, staring up at his face while he pushes inside me, just an inch.

He gazes down at me, our eyes locked, then he thrusts gently again, another inch.

My hands run up his arms, tracing the rigid muscles and then clenching on his shoulders.

Eyes still on mine, he drives in fully in one deep lunge and we both groan.

He blows out a breath and then his head dips, our foreheads touching. His mouth strokes against mine, a tender touch, and then we're kissing while he slides in and out, slowly. I memorize the taste of his lips, his tongue against mine, the press of his hips.

He moves, driving into me in metered strokes, advancing and retreating, layering pleasure atop pleasure, heat chasing over my skin and sensitizing every touch of his body against mine.

Desire builds and builds. He moves faster, sensing the coming finale. He shifts closer, pushing his body exactly where I need it. That's all it takes for me to splinter into a thousand fragments of bliss.

Jake shouts, shuddering, his arms tightening around me before he collapses, his weight pressing me into the mattress.

A tear leaks out of the corner of my eye, escaping into the cotton bedspread.

After a moment he rolls to the side, getting up to get rid of the condom before returning and drawing me back into his arms.

I clutch at him. I don't want this, whatever it is, to be over.

How can I leave? But how can I stay?

Chapter Twenty-Two

RYAN

"Don't move back to New York for Jake. Move for you. Jake is just, like, a perk."

I rest my elbows on the cluttered desk, holding my face in my hands. "Are you trying to get rid of me?"

Bernie taps on her keyboard. "No. I want you to be happy. Even if it's not with me."

"I am happy," I grumble.

She snorts. "Yeah. You sound ecstatic."

I came by the hospital to settle the rest of Mom's accounts and dropped by Bernie's office in the basement to say hi.

I'm now regretting that decision.

Bernie picks up her pen, tapping it on a notepad in front of her. "What does Ari think?"

I groan and rub my face. "She refuses to unpack from our trip." We've been back home for two weeks now. "If I told her I was even thinking about moving anywhere near Whitby, she'd start walking and meet me there."

Jake and I have been chatting and texting throughout the day, every day, and then we do a video call with Ari every night.

It's not enough.

It's almost worse, seeing him, talking to him, and not touching him.

But I can't move across the country for a man.

"Here." Bernie clicks around and the printer behind me buzzes to life. She points to it. "Grab that."

I sigh but comply. "What is this?" My eyes scan down the page.

"A list of nursing programs within two hours of Whitby, along with each school's requirements and due dates for applications."

The words blur in front of my eyes.

"Not to pressure you or anything, but some of them start interviews in August for spring admission, so the apps are due real soon."

I blink to clear my vision. "I don't even . . . how can I?"

"How can you not?"

What if they don't accept me? What if they do? How can I afford it? I would need a job and a place to live. I would have to move my whole life, and Ari's, thousands of miles.

I've done it before, but I didn't have a child then.

"I could come visit you. I love New York. Just think about it."

I blow out a breath. "Ugh."

"You miss all the shots you don't take."

I roll my eyes, an exaggerated motion.

"We do things not because they are easy, but because they are hard."

"Okay, Yogi Berra, I get it, all right? I'll think about it."

I push myself to stand and head for the door.

"Oh, one more thing," Bernie calls out. "You know that charity that paid that chunk of your mom's bill?"

I turn to look at her, lifting my brows, my hand on the door handle.

"That wasn't a charity. That was Jake."

"Why didn't you tell me?" I'm sitting on my bed with the door shut, on a video call with Jake.

"It was a gift. I didn't want you to know because I knew you wouldn't accept it. You wouldn't even let me buy you groceries. I told Elaine not to tell you. Please don't be upset. I wanted to do it." He winces. "Did I totally screw up again?"

I blow out a breath. I should be mad. He lied by omission, again. And yet . . .

"Paying off part of my mom's medical bills and not

telling me was a kind gesture. I just don't know how I can ever pay you back."

I'm not used to accepting help. Why is it so hard?

"I don't want you to pay me back." His eyes brighten. "Wait. You could pay me back by moving here and helping Finley."

I chuckle. "Helping Finley?"

"She's been interviewing for all these part-time manager positions for the camp, and it's been an absolute nightmare. The last guy showed up in a dirty shirt, unshowered, and smelling like he just smoked ten pounds of weed."

"That sucks."

"It does. But it's good, because you would be perfect for the job."

I scratch the back of my neck. It's actually not a terrible idea. Especially if it's part-time. Especially since I would need something part-time if I got into any of the nursing programs on the list Bernie gave me.

Before I can muster any kind of reply, Ari bursts into the room and jumps on the bed next to me, squeezing into the camera frame. "Jake!"

"Hey, superhero." He grins at her.

She jumps around, hands flapping behind her. "Look at my new cape."

"It's incredible."

She stops hopping around. "When are you coming to visit?"

"Soon."

I hand her the phone so she can talk Jake's ear off for a few minutes until he has to say goodbye. It's only seven here, but it's ten in New York and he's taking a group of campers on a hike early the next morning.

After we hang up with Jake, I don't want to move. So, I don't.

Ari sits next to me, leaning into my side. "I want to see Jake."

She says this a lot. It's become almost more frequent than *why*. I never thought I would prefer the *why*s.

"When can we go visit Jake again? And Oliver?"

I put an arm around her. "You liked it there?"

She taps my leg with her fingers. "Yep."

"What would you think if we lived there, permanently?"

"What is perm-ently?"

"Like, what if we lived there forever?"

She purses her lips. "I would miss my friends. But we could email and FaceTime."

"Right."

She pats me on the head. "I'm very young. I'll adapt."

I snort out a laugh. "Where did you hear that?"

"YouTube."

"Of course."

Chapter Twenty-Three

JAKE

It's a beautiful summer day in June. It isn't too hot or too cold. The air is fresh and clean, like sunshine and dirt and growing things. The wind whispers through the leaves in the trees overhead.

And I'm surrounded by twenty middle schoolers and freaking depressed as hell.

We're gathered along a hiking trail. Atticus is up at the front of the group, explaining some kind of creepy-looking mushroom thing to the kids, while Archer and I bring up the rear.

Moving usually helps with depression, something I learned from my sobriety journey. Just keep moving your body. Get the blood flowing. It makes a difference. Not today.

Atticus drones on and on. Damn, he loves his mushrooms.

The kid in front of us shifts, bumping into his companion, who turns and shoves him back.

"Hey." The mere sound of Archer's deep baritone is enough to make them stiffen and apologize.

It probably helps that he's six foot five and built like a damn mountain.

I sigh.

Is Atticus seriously still talking about mushrooms?

He must sense the crowd getting restless because he finally stops jabbering on about fungi and we keep moving.

"How are Ryan and Ari?" Archer asks.

I shrug my backpack up higher. "They're good."

"How are you?"

I breathe in some fresh air. It's not helping. "I don't know, man. It's hard. I miss them. I know I've only known them for a few weeks. Is that weird?"

He jumps over a log in the path. "Nah. I knew the first time I saw your sister that she would be important to me."

"Really?"

The path narrows. He steps ahead of me, talking over his shoulder. "Yep. You were throwing up in Veronica's parking lot and she was trying to carry you while being honked at and laughing her ass off."

I grimace. "Not my finest hour."

I don't even remember it. The things I put Finley

through. I'm lucky she didn't kick my ass or kick me out of our house completely. She would have been well within her rights. I would have deserved it.

Archer comes to an abrupt halt, spinning around to face me. "Hey. You've been through hell, and you came through like a fucking champion." He puts a hand on my shoulder. "I am proud of you."

I swallow back a lump forming in my throat. Damn, I'm emotional today. Lack of sleep.

"Thanks, man. Having you and Finley in my corner, it changed my life."

He slaps me on the back a couple of times and then turns around and keeps walking.

We pick up speed to catch up with the slower-moving group.

After a few minutes of walking, I tell him, "You were right, you know."

"About what?"

"What you said in the hospital when you and Finely first got together."

He turns his head to talk over his shoulder. "What words of wisdom did I impart to you? I honestly don't remember."

"You said grief is the price we pay for love and given the choice between grief and nothing, you'd choose grief every time."

"Huh. I sure am smart."

I chuckle. "Yeah, smart-ass. But . . . it's why I might have to move."

He stops again, turning and facing me. "You'll move there?"

"If she won't move here. I've been looking at real estate nearby. If I'm going to convince her to move in with me, I want to have some kind of plan. A place of our own. I'm going to head out to visit this weekend instead of in two weeks like we planned." I also want to bring Shirley back to Ari. I found the toy the day after they left. The rabbit was tucked up in between the wall and the mattress of the bottom bunk bed. "I want to surprise her and Ari and try to convince her to move. If that doesn't work . . ." I shrug. I have to do it. I would move mountains for my girls.

He twists his lips. "I don't like it, but I get it."

"She's worth it."

"I'm glad. And you know Finley will just commandeer Oliver's jet every other day if she wants to see you. But for what it's worth, I'm really hoping you can convince her to come here."

"Me too."

~

I practice various speeches the entire flight into Portland. I make a whole list of reasons New York is better than Oregon. I search for quotes about journeys and new beginnings and . . . love.

I haven't told Ryan I love her, but I do. I love her and Ari. I need to tell her. Them. Will it be enough?

What if she doesn't want to move to New York and also doesn't want me to move to Dull?

I know she cares about me but . . . what if she's changed her mind?

By the time I get off the plane and into the rental car, I'm nearly bursting with anticipation and anxiety.

I texted Ryan this morning to find out what their schedule would be like today so I could show up when they got home from all their activities and obligations. It works out, because even leaving New York in the morning, because of the time change, I don't arrive until midafternoon, then I have to drive two hours to Dull.

By the time I get there, it's near dinner time.

Ari is in front of their house, drawing on the sidewalk.

She looks up when I pass by, and when she spots me behind the wheel, she drops her chalk and jumps to her feet waving and yelling.

There must be a renter in my old place, because there isn't any parking on the cul-de-sac.

I drive to the end and flip around. I'll have to park somewhere on the cross street. I stop by Ari and roll down the window. "Hey, there superhero."

"Jake, you're here!" She's hopping up and down with excitement, chalk all over her clothes, her hair in wild disarray.

Lightness fills me, a sense of buoyancy chasing out the gloom of the past week.

"I've got to find a place to park the car. I'll be right back, okay?"

She nods, still jumping around.

Chuckling, I drive forward and halt at the stop sign, waiting for a few cars to pass, before pulling out onto the street and spotting a space halfway down the block.

I'm grabbing my overnight bag and Shirley from the trunk when Ari's voice reaches me over the hum of traffic.

I glance in her direction. She's on her scooter, racing down the sidewalk.

Frowning, I shut the trunk. What is she doing?

She hops the curb, riding into the road without looking.

Alarm shoots through me. I check the street, my blood turning into ice. A car is barreling toward her, a small black sedan.

Do they see her?

Fear clutches me in a tight grip, the air whooshing out of my lungs. *No.* They aren't slowing down.

"Ari!" I drop my bag and sprint.

Time is the enemy. It kicks into overdrive. My ears ring. I can't force my legs hard enough or fast enough. She's so close, but too far away. With barely a second to spare, I shove her out of the way.

Did I push too hard? Is she okay?

A flash of white-hot pain collides with my ribs, the blunt force ricocheting through my whole body, followed by pitch black.

Chapter Twenty-Four

JAKE

"Come on Jake, we have to go."

"We don't *have* to do anything."

Aria flips onto her side to face me. "I heard Taylor talking to Tiffany and she said anyone and everyone will be there. That means we have to be there."

My stomach churns with dread. "We can't go."

Aria pokes me in the side. "Jake."

"No."

She pokes me again. "Jaaaaake," she sing-songs.

"It's a bad idea."

"Uh, actually it's the best idea we've had."

"You've had."

"You, me, we, it's all the same." She lifts a hand, gesturing between us.

Her eyes scan over me, dark and almond shaped, just like mine. Her nose, a petite replica of my own, scrunches in thought.

She flops back on the bed, her long hair spreading out on the black and white bedspread. The scent of her hair, the jasmine shampoo she loves, hits me right in the gut. Why does my whole body hurt?

Her hand reaches for mine. "It wasn't your fault, Jake."

A high-pitched ringing reverberates in my ears. "What?"

It's like I've been shoved into a glass jar and someone's banging on the lid.

My fifteen-year-old self dissipates like smoke, and memories rush back in.

This memory, and all that followed.

Terror

Loss.

Grief.

Guilt.

And the pain. The all-consuming pain.

My vision goes black. A faint beep echoes in the distance. What is that?

I blink. No. I have to stay here with her. She can't go. I can't go. Not yet.

"Aria?"

Her hand squeezes mine.

The sensation pulls me back into her room. The heat

of her fingers. The soft pads pressing onto the back of my hand. The familiarity.

I blink harder, and my vision clears.

I'm still in Aria's room, on her bed. Everything exactly as it was the week before she died.

"Am I really talking to you, or is this just my subconscious talking to itself?"

Her head tilts toward me. "Does it matter?"

"I don't know. Maybe?"

I can't stop staring at her. This is so real. She looks exactly as I remember, down to the freckle on her neck. I miss her so much that the pain nearly takes my breath away.

"I don't want to forget you."

She shrugs. "Then don't."

I try to swallow, but my throat is sore. "It's so hard to remember."

She sighs. "Because you are so focused on forgetting. Stop it. You have to forgive yourself."

"It's not that simple."

She frowns at me. "If you had died, and I had lived, would you want me to be miserable?"

"Of course not."

She snaps her fingers. "I've got it. What if I forgive you? Right here, right now."

"But this is my dream. Wouldn't that be the same as me forgiving myself?"

"Is there really a difference?"

I am so confused. "I don't know."

"You have to surrender."

I don't understand. "To what?"

She lifts a hand. "Everything. Let go of the guilt, so you can hold on to the memories. The good things. I want you to keep those close and release the dark things that no longer matter."

"How? It's so hard."

"You just have to choose to do it, every day, decide to let it go until it becomes second nature."

This sounds familiar. "One day at a time."

Her eyes lock with mine. "It won't be perfect. You'll fail, sometimes. It's all right. It took you twelve years to walk into the forest. It's going to take some time and effort to walk out."

My body aches. The room dims, then brightens again. "How do you just surrender and release it? I can't. If I drop that rope, I'm dropping you along with it."

"The opposite is true."

My vision goes hazy. My heart is a drumbeat in my ears, my head throbbing. "I don't know if I can let go of the guilt. You were just a child."

"Jake." She reaches over, shaking my shoulder. "You were just a child too. Remember?" She points between the two of us. "Twins."

The room is getting darker again, her face blurring in front of me. "Don't go."

"I'm always here, Jake. I never went anywhere." Her

voice is fading. "Forgive yourself. Think of all the good we had. Jake, *remember me*."

The room disappears in a blink.

I open my eyes.

Chapter Twenty-Five

RYAN

I'm so sick of hospitals.

But I'm also not leaving until Jake wakes up.

"Anything yet?" Finley whispers from the doorway, her face stark, eyes shadowed with fatigue. She steps into the room, her gaze roving over Jake, asleep in his bed, and then moving to Ari, passed out in a cot next to him.

"Not yet. Hopefully soon."

The doctor told us yesterday he should be waking up at any minute.

I rub my thumb over his hand.

"Did you want to sit with him?" I shift in the chair, ready to stand.

"No. It's fine." Her brows crease. "Have you slept at all?"

I shake my head. "No. I can't."

She clucks in sympathy. "I get it. I'll be back, I'm going to let the others know."

She disappears and I stare at Jake's face. Willing him to open his eyes, as I've been doing every minute for the past fourteen hours.

All in all, he got lucky. The driver of the car braked at the last minute, so the speed was greatly reduced when the impact occurred. Jake was knocked off his feet, cracked some ribs, has a crap ton of bruises, and hit his head against the pavement.

They did an MRI and determined there was no brain bruising or bleeding, and the concussion is mild, but he hasn't woken up.

Maybe it's because of the pain meds.

Ari scraped her hands and knees on the pavement when Jake shoved her out of the way, but was otherwise unharmed. Emotionally, she was a wreck, terrified, racked with guilt, certain she had been the cause of Jake getting hurt.

She couldn't contain herself. She was so excited to see him. She knows to look both ways, but she's only six.

I had been on the porch watching her only a minute before the whole thing went down. I went inside to use the bathroom, and when I came out, Ari was gone. I ran out into the street and came across the whole scene right after it happened.

I should have made her come inside while I peed, but I had no idea Jake would show up, no idea she would run out into the street after him, no idea there would be a teenage kid driving down the road, not paying attention.

The ambulance arrived within minutes, whisking both Ari and Jake away.

The driver was also beside himself with guilt.

The whole thing was a series of unfortunate events.

But no one was seriously injured, so all in all . . . it will be okay.

I just wish he would open his eyes and then I might believe it.

It's probably better that he rest and heal.

His entire family, all four sisters and their significant others, arrived about six hours ago. After crowding the room for a few minutes, they set up camp in the waiting area and have been taking turns coming in to check on him.

They've been wonderful. I've been hugged more in the past six hours than I have the rest of my entire life. They brought us food, insisting we eat something. All of their care and assurances are the only reason Ari was able to finally fall asleep.

I wish I could join her. I'm exhausted and yet wired. I lean forward and rest my head next to Jake's hand.

Maybe I'll just shut my eyes for a minute.

Jake's fingers twitch against mine and I jerk up, eyes flying up to lock with his.

He's awake.

My heart tumbles in my chest.

His smile is crooked. "Hey you. Surprise."

I burst into tears.

He shifts in the bed, trying to move. I put a hand up to stop him and try to pull myself together, wiping at my face. "I'm okay," I manage. "I was so worried."

He winces. "What happened?" Then his eyes widen, his whole body going tense. "Ari. Where is she?"

"She's fine," I assure him. "She's asleep." I gesture toward the cot on the other side of his bed.

He looks over and then relaxes, slumping back into the bed. His hand squeezes mine. "Tell me everything."

I give him the rundown of the accident, how his whole family is here waiting for him to wake up, how no one was injured except for him, and his injuries are not major, and everything is fine. At least it will be, once his bruising heals.

"I'm sorry." His voice is hoarse.

I grab the cup of water from the side table and hold the straw to his mouth. "What are you sorry for? None of this was your fault."

He drinks some water and settles back in the bed. "I wanted to surprise you and Ari. I should have been paying more attention to her when I was parking."

"Jake, you saved her. I am the one who should have been paying more attention. I shouldn't have left her alone."

"It's not your fault. It's no one's fault. I," he blinks rapidly, "I dreamed about Aria."

Surprised by the sudden change in subject, I lean forward. "What?"

"I was in Aria's room with her, and we were talking, and it was a real conversation we had before she died, only it was different." His gaze grows distant. "She told me to forgive myself."

"She's right."

His eyes lift to mine. "I didn't mean to forget her."

"You didn't forget her."

He swallows. "But I wanted to."

I shake my head. "That was only because you were hurting. You'll remember. And we have a whole box of memories of her, the letters your dad wrote me."

"We do."

"I can read them with you. We can remember together if you want."

One corner of his mouth kicks up. "You will?"

"I might be living close, pretty soon."

His eyes widen. "Really?"

"I may have a list of places near Whitby with nursing schools, which Bernie gave me the other day before you arrived."

He grins. "I knew I liked her. When are you moving?"

I chuckle. "I haven't even applied yet, let alone looked for places to live. I haven't come up with any kind of plan to make anything work."

His smile doesn't dim in the slightest. "But you will."

"I might not get accepted again at Cornell."

His fingers twitch in mine. "You will."

"You don't know that."

"If you don't get in there, you can apply to other places. Or reapply next semester. And in the meantime, you can live with me. I've been making a list too, of available real estate near Whitby."

My stomach dips. He has? "It's not too soon?"

He shrugs, but then winces. "Who decides what's too soon?"

"Jake?" Ari sits up in the cot, her voice thick with sleep.

"Hey, superhero."

She immediately scrambles off the cot.

He lifts his arm and she climbs up next to him, settling into his side.

"Careful," I say.

Jake tugs her closer. "She's fine."

Ari blinks at me with bleary eyes. "Are we gonna live with Jake?"

"I don't know, baby." I meet Jake's eyes. "I would need a job or something."

"You have any experience in property management?" Finley asks from the doorway. "I've been on the hunt for another manager to hire, even if it's part-time, to take over some of my duties. I want to focus on teaching ice skating, not to mention my upcoming wedding. I'm looking for someone who doesn't totally suck and it will be a bonus if you're good with kids." She winks.

Then the whole group of them tumble into the room.

"Look who finally decided to wake up," Oliver says, his tone as dry as the desert.

"Have a nice nap, princess?" Archer adds.

Finley moves around the bed to the side I'm sitting on. "Sorry to butt in. We weren't trying to eavesdrop."

Piper is right behind her. "Right. We weren't *trying* anything, we were just doing."

"But seriously, we need to talk about this job opportunity," Finley says to me in a low voice.

The next half hour is noisy chaos, Jake's family assuring themselves he is, in fact, okay, and then a nurse comes in and kicks everyone out.

He's going to be discharged later today after the doctor clears him. He'll need to take it easy for a bit since his ribs will take four to six weeks to fully heal.

We say goodbye to his family, and I promise to take care of Jake. They are flying back to New York tonight.

Once they're gone, it's just Jake and Ari and me.

"So. Have you thought about it?"

I adjust his blanket. "Thought about what?"

"Momma," Ari says, annoyed, "are we going to move to New York with Jake or what?"

I chuckle. The sass on this one is unreal sometimes. "I'm not sure. What do you think?"

"I think it makes sense."

I choke back a laugh. "You might be right."

Jake's smile is blinding. "I'll stay here with you while things are sorted out and I'm recovering. I'll have a lot of time to make phone calls, help you with whatever you need that doesn't involve heavy lifting, and get things in motion for us to go back to New York together. Finley might be calling you daily about working with her, so be prepared for a lot of pressure and probably some guilt trips."

Emotions bubble up. I can't believe we're talking about this. I can't believe this will happen.

"Hey." Jake looks down at Ari and then over at me. "It's a lot. We have a lot to think about, a lot to do, but . . . I love you. I love you both. We got this together, okay?"

Ari stares up at him. "Okay."

I blink, trying not to cry. I lean forward to press my lips to his. "I love you too."

"Me too!" Ari wiggles, planting a slightly wet kiss on my cheek before giving Jake's chin similar treatment.

Jake's laughing eyes meet mine. In that second, it hits me. It doesn't matter how hard the journey ahead may be. It holds little weight compared to what we've both been through, the sequence of events that brought us here to this moment, together.

Whatever happens next, we have each other.

Epilogue

JAKE

The plow bounces over a snow drift and Ari whoops in the seat next to me, lifting her arms in the air like we're riding a roller coaster. "Go faster!"

I chuckle. "Pretty sure this thing tops out at thirty-five."

Not to mention the fact that it's still pitch-black outside and the twinkle lights are muted with snow.

Ari woke up at five this morning.

When we were kids, it was the same every Christmas. Aria woke me at the crack of dawn, always too excited about all the presents under the tree to sleep in past six.

Ryan is still sleeping, so I bundled up Ari and took her out to plow away some of the snow that fell over the camp last night.

I'm trying to keep her distracted until it's late enough to meet up with the rest of our family.

"I think we're about done." At least, the main road that winds through the camp has been taken care of.

I spin the wheel, turning the plow around. "What do you say we head back and have some hot cocoa?" And I can brew up some coffee. A jolt or twelve of caffeine is exactly what I need.

"Do we have marshmallows and whipped cream?"

I press a hand to my chest, feigning offense. "Do I look like a cocoa amateur?"

She laughs.

I come to a stop in front of our cabin, the same one Finley always sets aside for us, the one we stayed in a year and a half ago during Ryan and Ari's first visit to Camp Aria.

Ari scoots across the bench seat to get out on my side, and I lift her out and down to the slick snow. "Be careful."

"I will." She scampers up the walkway to the cabin, not careful in the slightest.

I sigh and follow her inside, hanging our coats and scarves up on the rack in the entryway, exposing our matching Christmas pajamas. Finley bought coordinating sets for the entire family, all red flannel and green stripes. The woman is a menace. But Ari does look pretty adorable and she absolutely loved the fact that the whole family matches.

Ari hops up on the stool at the kitchen island. "Can we go to the big house after cocoa?"

I glance over at the clock. It's six. "Maybe? I'm sure by the time your mom wakes up and gets ready it will be time to go. How does that sound?"

"Good."

Oliver and Piper are more than likely up and about. Their son, Jonathon, is only ten months old and doesn't sleep past seven. I move around the kitchen, pushing the button on the coffee machine and grabbing the milk from the fridge for the cocoa.

Finley is probably awake too. She was just as excited about Christmas as Ari. It's not often she manages to gather the whole family in the same spot at the same time, and the mountain of presents under the tree is mostly a result of her efforts.

Everyone is eager to see Ari's reaction to the gift I got her.

Anticipation twists in my stomach. I really hope she likes it.

We drove in from Binghampton yesterday morning. We've been renting a house there for almost a year now. Binghampton sits in between Whitby and Ithaca, an hour away in either direction. Ryan started classes at Ithaca last spring. She's also been helping Finley part-time with a variety of tasks in her downtime, some of which she can do from home—like payroll and accounting. Most of our weekends are spent at the camp anyway, much to Ari's delight.

Yesterday after we arrived, we rode on snowmobile, went ice skating, and built snowmen, and then after dinner, we played Uno and charades with everyone.

The milk steams, and I remove it from the heat, pouring it into the mug. I stir in the chocolate and marshmallows and add a dollop of whipped cream on top before setting it in front of Ari.

"Thank you." She picks up the spoon and shovels a giant bite of whipped cream into her mouth. "Daddy, do you think Santa knew to bring my presents here?"

My heart tumbles, the way it always does when she uses the moniker.

About eight months ago we were sitting on a bench in the early spring sunshine, enjoying ice cream cones after school when she asked if she could call me Daddy, since I was marrying her mommy. I told her yes, of course, and then had to change the subject so I wouldn't burst into tears like an infant.

I saved the crying for when Ryan came home and I was able to tell her the story in private and then sob on her shoulder.

Ryan and I aren't getting married until she's done with school. But I couldn't wait to ask her. I proposed one lazy morning in bed, shortly after we moved into our new place. Probably the least romantic proposal, since we were both naked at the time, but for some reason it was just . . . perfect.

"I'm sure Santa will find you. He knows when you're naughty and nice, he sees you when you're sleeping and all that, so clearly he must know you were sleeping here."

"Hmm." She purses her lips at me.

She's getting old enough to start questioning the whole Santa thing, but maybe we can squeeze out one more year before we have to break it to her—or the kids at school will.

I grab a couple mugs full of coffee. "You good?" I ask Ari. "I'm going to check on your mom, get her to start moving."

She nods. "I'm good."

Padding into the bedroom, I nudge the door with my foot, leaving it open a scant inch, and set our coffees down on the nightstand. Then I slip under the blankets, still warm with Ryan's body heat.

She immediately turns into me, one arm slipping around my waist, the other tucking between us. "Hmm," she murmurs, half asleep, her face settling into the crook of my neck, her nose brushing against my skin. "Jake."

I tighten my hold on her. "Merry Christmas."

Her lips slide against my neck. "How much time do we have?" Her voice is husky with sleep.

Within a split second, my cock hardens into a rock.

Damn. I will never get enough of this woman.

I stifle a groan. "Ari is awake. She's in the kitchen drinking hot cocoa."

"We need to soundproof these walls."

"Agreed. You should tell Finley that."

She chuckles, her laugh vibrating through me. My

heart squeezes inside my ribcage. I didn't know it was possible to be this deliriously happy.

"Can we go now?" Ari calls out from outside the door.

Ryan pulls back slightly. "Are you ready for this?" she asks, her voice low.

There's only one possible answer. "Yes."

Thirty minutes later, we walk into the main house using the side door that opens directly into the kitchen and I'm immediately struck with the scents of pine and cinnamon undercut with cleaning products. It smells like home. Laughter and the low hum of conversation drifts in from the living room.

"We're here!" Ari skips ahead of us.

Finley and Piper are both sitting on the floor, near Jonathon. The baby is standing at the coffee table in his flannel onesie, holding the edge and bobbing up and down. He's not walking quite yet, but he's getting the hang of moving around a bit while hanging on to something stable.

Oliver sits on the couch behind him next to Archer, his eyes focused on his son's every movement.

Luke and Mindy are in the recliner, Mindy snuggled into his lap.

"Where are Taylor and Ace?" I ask.

Ryan takes a seat on the couch next to Oliver and Archer. Ari settles on the floor between Finley and Piper.

"Taylor and Atticus should be here soon, they just woke up," Finley says.

I roll my eyes. "Shocker."

Mindy chuckles. "She's used to working late nights, but she knew it would be an early morning."

Holidays have always been especially tender, for all of us. Aria's absence is loud. But with Ari here, her youthful exuberance and innocence somehow provide a layer of relief.

"When can we open them?" Ari stares up at the tree, covered in multicolored lights and homemade ornaments mixed with store-bought bulbs in various colors.

It's not one of those perfect, catalogue-ready trees.

The tree itself was chopped down from the other side of the property. It's a little on the thin side, and there is a janky spot where the branches were uneven that Finley faced toward the wall.

Most of the decorations were made by all of us at various points in our childhoods. There is a clay mold of Aria's handprint up there, a drawing Piper did in kindergarten that someone poked a hole in and slipped through a string to hang on the tree, and a tinfoil star Aria and I made together. We wanted it to be a tree topper, but it wasn't sturdy enough.

It's not a perfect tree. It's messy. It's a tree full of life and memories, both good and sad.

It's perfect.

"Do you want to play elf and start handing out the presents? You can just put a pile to the side for when Taylor and Atticus get here, it should be any minute."

Ari jumps to her feet and races to the tree, vibrating with excitement at the permission to dig into the gifts.

I perch on the arm of the couch next to Ryan while Ari proceeds to sort and pile presents all around.

"I need an IV of coffee, stat!" Taylor calls from the kitchen, the door opening and shutting with their arrival.

"Hurry up, we're about to get started without you," Mindy yells back, shaking the gift in her hand that Ari just handed her.

Everyone has a small pile in front of them by the time Taylor and Atticus emerge from the kitchen, mugs in hand. They sit on the floor near Finley.

"Well, what are you waiting for? Dig in." Finley motions with a hand.

The sound of ripping paper fills the air as everyone opens at once, tossing ribbons and bows onto the floor.

Oliver has Jonathon in his lap, and he's holding up a T-shirt that reads *The Original* in block letters. Piper, laughing, holds up a baby-sized shirt that says *The Remix* in the same lettering.

"Jake, this is too much." Ryan's hand lands on my leg. She's staring down at the new laptop I bought for her.

"You need it for school."

She leans her head against my side. "Thank you."

I open the package in my lap. It's from Archer. It's a T-shirt with a photo on it. The photo is of me, sleeping, wrapped in the giant Archer face blanket.

I chuckle and look over to find him grinning at me.

"You're a di—uh," I glance over at Ari, clearing the bad word from my throat, "not nice person."

He just laughs, the dick.

Ari is still sorting through presents and handing them out, so interested in everyone else's gifts, she hasn't opened any of her own.

I make my way over to the tree to find a very specific box and bring it over to her.

"Here. Take a break from your elf duties and open this one." I set it in her hands and then crouch down next to her while she tears it open.

"It's a new backpack!"

"Open it up."

"There's more?"

"Yep." I swallow.

She opens the bag and pulls out a paper. "What is this?"

"Read it."

She scans over the page and then she reads the words slowly. "You may not have my eyes, you may not have my smile, but you have all of my heart. When you're ready, I would love the honor of being your real daddy." Her eyes fly up to mine.

The noise in the room has muted to almost nothing.

"Do you want to . . . adopt me?" Ari asks, her voice hushed.

"Of course, baby."

Her face crumples, her hands lifting to cover her eyes.

"Hey." I tug her onto my lap, her arms wrapping

around my neck, her face burrowing into my shoulder. "I love you, superhero."

"I love you too."

"There's no pressure here," I say into her hair. "It can take a long time to adopt, and if you need to think about it, that's okay. We can wait until you're older, we can talk about it again later, whatever you want. I just wanted you to know that I already consider you my daughter, and I always will. You will always be a part of my family. And if you ever want to make it official, we can do that."

Ryan sits next to me, her arms going around both of us.

After a minute I lift my head.

Finley swipes at her eyes.

Mindy is pressing a tissue to her nose.

Oliver holds Jonathon against his chest, his eyes gleaming.

Ari pulls back. "Does that mean I'll be family to everyone else here too?"

I wince. "I know that's a scary thought, but really they're not as bad as they seem. Don't let the thought of being related to," I wave a hand around, "all these weirdos scare you from making your decision."

She giggles and pushes on my chest. "Daddy!"

Archer chucks a wad of wrapping paper, smacking me right in the forehead.

"Way to ruin a moment." Taylor pitches a wad of ribbon at Archer.

The room turns into a full-scale battle, tissue paper

and bows and trimmings flying around the room indiscriminately.

Ari leaps out of my lap to join the fray.

Amidst the chaos, Ryan leans into my side.

I turn my head and brush a kiss over her mouth. She tastes like coffee and chocolate and home.

My eyes rove over her face, then over the rest of the room.

Archer is subduing Finley with one of his giant hands while batting away projectiles from Ari with the other. Mindy and Taylor have teamed up in a battle against Luke and Piper. Oliver is out of the line of fire, standing behind the couch, frowning at all of us. He's holding Jonathon against his chest to face the room, an identical scowl marring his little chunky baby face.

Happiness bubbles in my veins.

I shut my eyes and send out a quick prayer to my twin.

Thank you for bringing me to them.

I will always miss Aria. But I know that my grief is proof that love was here. It was real.

I open my eyes, my gaze locking with Ryan.

And love will continue.

The End.

~

If you or someone you know is in crisis, the link below will take you to a list of international hotlines. You can select your country of choice at the top, and it will provide a list of hotlines for everything from suicide prevention, to addiction, abuse, or domestic violence.

https://www.helpguide.org/find-help.htm

Also by Mary Frame

Imperfect Series:

Book One: Imperfect Chemistry

Book Two: Imperfectly Criminal

Book Three: Practically Imperfect

Book Four: Picture Imperfect

Book Five: Imperfect Strangers

Book Six: Imperfectly Delicious

The Dorky Duet (Plus a companion novel!)

Ridorkulous

Geektastic

Nerdelicious

Time after Time Series:

Time of My Life

If I Could Turn Back Time

Castle Cove Mystery Series

Fake It to the Limit

Too Much Crime on My Hands

You're the Con That I Want

Fox Family Series

Between a Fox and a Hard Place

The Fox and the Rebound

Another Fox Bites the Dust

Some Like It Fox

For Fox Sake

About the Author

Go here to sign up for the newsletter!
www.maryframe.com
Mary Frame is a full time mother and wife with a full time job. She has no idea how she manages to write novels, but it probably helps that she's a dedicated introvert. She doesn't enjoy writing about herself in third person, but she does enjoy reading, writing, dancing, and damaging the ear drums of her co-workers when she randomly decides to sing to them.

She lives in Reno, Nevada with her husband, two children, and a border collie named Stella.

She LOVES hearing from readers and will not only respond but likely begin stalking them while tossing out hearts and flowers and rainbows! If that doesn't creep you out, e-mail her at: maryframeauthor@gmail.com